Go Away!

The willow branches rustled, shedding droplets of water, as if the tree had straightened and shaken itself. Again, something reached out and touched him, chilling his bones. Steve stepped backwards, startled by his own fear.

At last he found his voice. "GO AWAY!" he shouted.

Other Point paperbacks
you will enjoy:

The Nightmare Man
by Tessa Krailing

All on a Winter's Day
by Lisa Taylor

Prom Dress
by Lael Littke

Party Line
by A. Bates

The Baby-sitter
by R.L. Stine

My Secret Admirer
by Carol Ellis

point

THE RAIN GHOST

Garry Kilworth

SCHOLASTIC INC.
New York Toronto London Auckland Sydney

ISBN 0-590-43415-2

Copyright © 1989 by Garry Kilworth. All rights reserved. Published by Scholastic Inc. by arrangement with Scholastic Publications Ltd., United Kingdom. POINT is a registered trademark of Scholastic Inc.

12 11 10 9 8 7 6 5 4 3 2   1 2 3 4 5/9

Printed in the U.S.A.   01

First Scholastic printing, March 1990

Chapter One

In the early morning there was a beheading. The executioner's blade was quick and clean, completing its work with a single stroke. It was over with hardly a sound. The severed bald pate dropped down on to the tabletop and lay with its flesh exposed. Steve Winston regarded it with utter distaste as he poked it with a teaspoon. "My egg's hard again!" he said.

His elder sister, Susan, shook her head sadly. "That'll teach you to chop the tops off your eggs with a knife. You're supposed to pat them with the spoon and then peel away the shell – not hack it to bits. Manners, chum, manners."

"I could smash it with a sledgehammer," he grumbled, "but that's not going to make the yolk soft, is it? What am I going to do with my Marmite soldiers now?" He tried stabbing one into the hard yoke and it broke in half. "Look at that. I gave it four minutes, like you said, straight from the fridge. Should've made it three, eh Benjy?"

Eight-month-old Benjamin squealed on hearing his name, then went back to the serious business of creating debris out of his breakfast. He was pre-occupied with scattering bits of soggy bread within a two metre radius of his high chair and it seemed he did not want to be distracted from this absorbing task. His little face had a grim expression of concentration as he first sucked the crust into limp submission and then whirled it off in some undeter-mined direction. A piece landed amongst Steve's Marmite soldiers: "Ben! it's about time you learned to aim that stuff properly . . ."

"Or even eat it," said Susan, descending on her infant son with damp flannel in hand.

Steve shovelled down the rest of his egg and then went upstairs to put on his school jacket and tie. At fourteen he was becoming fashion conscious, and though he had tried to modify his school uniform (yet remain inconspicuous to teachers) it still looked like a green blazer and grey flannels.

"Yuk," he grumbled, putting on his jacket, "bottle green. Might as well be a school for frogs. Why bottle green? Why not puce with yellow trimming?" He wasn't quite sure what colour puce was, but it sounded sicky.

His tie hung like a hangman's noose from the door handle, where he had draped it the evening before. He never undid it because the knot was special – a Windsor knot – and had been tied for him by Dave, the seventeen-year-old next door, who knew about these things. Steve was afraid that one day Susan would insist on washing the tie, and he would have to go back to Dave and admit that he could not remember the knotting sequence. So he never wore it down to breakfast, in case he got egg down it.

2

He sat down before the mirror and inspected his head. Hair gel ensured that the long blond bit of hair at the front curved out and down towards his eyes. Then there was an anxious inspection for spots, and one discovered near his nose. He turned the mirror over to the magnifying side, and investigated at ten times its normal magnitude. It looked horrendously inflamed, but there were aspects about its topography which served to dampen his initial alarm.

"Gnat bite," he said with relief. "Got to be." Mosquito bites were acceptable. It was blackheads and pimples that were enemies.

Steve studied the rest of his features. He had a long face, with a high Roman nose. He didn't like his face much, but since he was stuck with it, he realized he had to make the best of it. At least it stopped short of being horsey, like Philip Whiteman's. One of Steve's front teeth was crooked, and crossed the other, but this had recently become acceptable to him. He had heard Julie Parker, the girl he was madly in love with (at a distance) say she hated boys with perfect features– ". . . they look too soft".

Steve was pleased he had rugged teeth.

One day he intended to ask Graham, his best friend, to ask Rosemary, his next best friend (who just happened to be a girl, and not his girlfriend), to ask Julie Parker to come out with him. Asking Julie Parker directly was utterly impossible and requesting Rosemary's assistance as a go-between would be embarrassing, especially if Julie Parker said "no", as she was quite likely to do, and he had to hear it straight from Rosemary. Rosemary, he knew, disapproved of Julie Parker for some reason. Rosemary was not vindictive, but she could wear an I-told-you-so expression better than anyone Steve knew. So he needed this double buffer between himself and the girl who turned his guts to warm butter.

When Steve had stopped studying himself in the mirror he went to the window to look for Graham. It was a bright spring day. His friend was just sauntering along the unmade road, taking swipes at roses overhanging garden walls with his Adidas bag. Petals showered the pathway.

Steve opened the window, leaned out, and yelled, "Got the D&D stuff?"

Graham looked blank for a minute, then began checking his bag for the Dungeons and Dragons chart, dice, character book and personal figures. They would need them during the fourth lesson when M. Lafarge, the French teacher let them play the game, so long as they used *Chroniques d'Outre Monde*, the French role-playing magazine. Graham was the current Dungeon Master, his character role Le Loup, the wolf.

Presumably it was all there, because he gave the thumbs up sign and then tapped significantly at his watch, warning Steve of the time. Both boys lived in Paglesham, a village situated on the coastal strip of East Anglia. Paglesham had the Thames estuary to the south, the sea to the east, and a marsh area known locally as "the dengies" to the north. The nearest town was Rochford, where the boys went to school. Even with the windows and doors all closed, the odours of the creeks and backwaters of the marshes permeated the house: the tangy scents of bladder-wrack, saltwort, and the slightly less overpowering sea lilac. When the tide was out, and the crazed networks of slickmud channels were exposed to a hot sun, Whopper said the smell became so thick you could lean on it and not fall over. Whopper had once

4

been the local smuggler and, at eighty, was Paglesham's oldest inhabitant. He now spent most of his time in The Plough and Sail, attempting to drink more cognac than he had ever managed to smuggle across the Channel in his youth.

It was Whopper who had told Steve, Graham and Rosemary about Brandy Hole, the largest creek on the river Crouch, and they frequently went into its labyrinth of channels in their canoes.

Steve went downstairs again, just in time to catch Jack, his sister's husband, doing his usual whirlwind act. "No time, no time," cried Jack, heading towards the door, still eating his bowl of cornflakes. Every morning the residents of Paglesham Eastend witnessed Jack hurrying along the dirt road, navigating potholes, and spooning down cornflakes. He would hide the spoon and empty bowl under a bush, near where he caught the bus to Southend. Jack was always in a rush to get somewhere on time, and was invariably late by about two minutes. It was only because the local bus service ran on similar lines that Jack managed to get to work at all. Jack was always late, the bus was always late, and thus they coincided.

"Steve," said Susan, halfway through changing Ben's nappy, "would you pick up the bowl on the way home tonight? Jack will forget."

"This is a nutty household," said Steve. "When Mum was . . ." he stopped and looked at the floor.

Susan stared at him for a moment and then said. "You don't mind, do you?"

Steve shook his head. " 'Course not, sis. Watch out, Benjy's got the . . ."

Benjamin's elastic arm had reached out and toppled the milk bottle, which was fortunately almost empty.

It went rolling across the floor, spilling milk on the tiles.

"What was it doing on the floor," groaned Susan.

"Jack was giving some to the cat."

Steve picked up the bottle, put it on the table, and then made for the door. He paused in the doorway. "I'm thinking of having a black streak," he said quickly.

His sister looked up from powdering Benjamin's bottom. "Think again, buster. Your hair stays as it is."

Steve kicked lightly but petulantly at the door jamb. "Please, sis. Mum and Dad would have let me."

"Mum and Dad are not here. We're your legal guardians – Jack and me."

"That doesn't mean . . ."

Susan straightened up. "Look, Stevie, Mum and Dad might have let you, but that's not the point. We have to be stricter than they were, otherwise we'll get all sorts of people round here telling us how to manage our lives. I know dyeing your hair is not the end of the world. I'm only twenty-three myself – think I've forgotten what it's like? Jack would probably say yes, but I'm asking you not to do it. I don't want to – to attract attention to us."

Steve was disappointed. Of course, he could go ahead and get the black streak in his blond hair, but he did not want to upset his sister. "Okay," he said resignedly.

She gave him a brief smile and then asked, "Who's the girl anyway? Rosemary?"

He felt his face going hot. "Rosemary is a friend of mine. Can't boys have friends amongst the opposite sex?"

Susan smiled again and shrugged. "Just asking."

She went back to giving her attention to Benjamin.

Once outside, Steve saw that Graham was hopping from one foot to the other. He was shorter than Steve, but stockier, with broad shoulders and a square face. He wore John Lennon glasses, but, unlike most boys of his age who wore spectacles, did not look bookish. The glasses looked out of place on a face that was usually seen dashing around in some competitive sport. Graham was a good all-rounder with special talents in swimming and high diving. Steve was a good swimmer too, and a fair tennis player, but no match for Graham in either sport. Still, at least he didn't have to wear glasses.

The two boys were silent as they made their way to the bus stop. The school bus was chugging away, coughing out fumes, waiting for them. They climbed on board, and went to the back where Rosemary was waiting for them, saving two seats. She was always the first on the bus.

As they passed, "Gibbo" Gibson, the boy grabbed Steve's sleeve and sneered, "When you goin' to get up in the morning's Winston Churchill? We've been sittin' waiting for you for half an hour."

Steve was a little afraid of Gibbo. He wrenched his sleeve away.

"I'm *talkin*' to you, lanky."

"What do you want me to say?" said Steve. "Sorry? You don't want to get to school any more than anyone else does."

"That's my business, not yours . . ."

Rosemary shouted, "You're wasting more time, Alan Gibson."

Gibson coloured. Steve knew that hard as the young farm boy was, he could not handle comments from girls. What was also obvious was that he fancied Rosemary.

7

Steve went to the back to join his friends. There was also the unvoiced knowledge that Gibbo was wary, if not actually afraid, of Graham. But Steve's friend would never intervene on his behalf. It wasn't done. It was bad enough that Rosemary insisted on doing so, but it was better than having Graham for a bodyguard. That would have been too humiliating for words.

Rosemary was an attractive, slightly sturdy-looking girl with a round face and sea-blue eyes. Unlike the boys she was fiercely academic and outshone them in the classroom in virtually all subjects. Her grandfather had been a Dutch engineer who, along with many others, had settled in Paglesham after helping to claim areas of salt marsh from the sea. Many of the creek dykes and sea walls had her grandfather's mark on their crowstones.

"Did you remember the D&D?" she said to Graham.

"What D&D?" he said, looking puzzled, and she punched him on the arm until he said in a Mexican accent culled from TV westerns, "Of course, senyou-reeta, but deed you remember the fish?"

"Feesh?" cried Steve. "I don' wan' your steenking feesh."

Rosemary ignored them. "Well L'épervier is going to make it to the treasure before any of your pathetic warriors, so stink all you want."

"I got to hand it to you Babe," said Steve, copying Renko from "Hill Street Blues", "you're just the best damn cop on the hill, even if you are a strawberry blonde with a creamy complexion and can't handle a mature relationship . . ."

"Don't you two ever stop?" she laughed.

"Nope," said Steve with a James Stewart lisp, "can't

say as we hardly do, ma'am." He reverted to his normal voice. "Anyway, you're only getting through the Cave de Chan so well because you have a high orientation factor – wait until brute force is needed. There's no one to beat Thrang Noir when it comes to fighting."

"What about des Gobelins last week. They nearly did for you there, Thrang."

"I had the situation in hand," replied Steve.

The school bus arrived outside Sweyn's Comprehensive School and the children disembarked with their usual noise. Steve stepped down from the bus and the three friends crossed into the playground. Gibbo met up with his cronies and muttered something to them. They all glared at Steve, who tried not to feel uncomfortable. This had been a regular scenario since he had arrived at senior school, so he wasn't all that worried. In fact, the hostility had begun at junior school, when his mother and father were alive. Then his parents had been killed, not long after he had started at Sweyn's, in a car accident on the M4.

Rosemary left the two boys to go across and talk to Julie Parker. Steve felt himself going all hot. Well, it was Friday and he would have to make the most of today, because there would be two weekend days when he could not sit and drool over her. Once again, he wondered whether to ask Graham to ask Rosemary to ask Julie . . . but shook his head fiercely. Not yet. Not yet.

"What's the matter with your head?" asked Graham.

"Nothing," said Steve. "Thought there was a wasp or something."

The bell rang and they reluctantly dragged themselves up the steps towards the assembly hall.

Chapter Two

A Saturday morning in spring! Steve opened his eyes as he heard the magpies screeching at each other on the roof. Saturday morning – the best time of the week. If only all days were as good as Saturday. Clump, clump, clump; the magpies were wearing hobnail boots. They were toughs of the birdworld, magpies. Steve had seen them divebombing cats and chasing squirrels from the garden. Magpies would put the boot in, put the beak in, soon as look at you, he thought. They strutted, bounded across the lawn, even put the jays in their place and jays were no slouches when it came to punchups. Gibbo magpies.

He sat up in bed. Pinned to the bedroom walls around him were colourful pictures of Japanese motorcycles, mostly Hondas, Yamahas and Kawasakis. There were also several monochrome magazine photos of ancient British bikes: BSAs, Nortons, Triumphs. One day Steve would own a motorbike. One or two of the kids at school already had track bikes, which they rode on farmland. At the moment there was no question: apart from everything else, there was no money available for such luxuries. He had not even bothered to talk to Susan about it. He knew what her reaction would be and why start an argument for nothing? Sometimes he liked to stir things up a bit, but not over something as important as this.

"What are you doing today?" asked Susan, as he went into the kitchen looking for some breakfast.

"Gray and Rosemary and me are going canoeing. Is that okay? Did you want any jobs done?" He stared through the window. Jack was haring up and down the lawn with a mower, a piece of toast stuck in his mouth. By ten o'clock Jack would have a dozen jobs done, while other people were just thinking about opening the newspaper. By midday, he would be exhausted and lying on the lawn with the baby asleep on his chest.

"No, no jobs, but don't leave your homework until the last minute," warned his sister. "Last Sunday evening you were up until midnight."

"That was a special project. I haven't got much this weekend. I know I always say that, but this weekend it's true. In fact I'll do it now, before I go out."

His sister did a mock faint. "Perhaps I ought to call the doctor?" she said.

Steve ignored her and went back upstairs to get his school books. It was true that he hadn't got a great deal to do, and last Monday he had hardly been able to keep his eyes open in class. He made a vow then that he would get it done *before* the weekend, then feel free for the next two days. He got himself some cornflakes and then sat at the table.

"Maths," he groaned to himself.

An hour later, Susan came into the room with Benjamin tucked under one arm. Jack was close behind. It was his turn to change the child's nappy and Ben was looking alarmingly satisfied with himself.

"Pongo-pongo nappy," said Susan, wrinkling her nose.

"*Two* pongos," Jack cried in dismay, "that means it's a bad one."

"I had a three-er the other day," said Steve, "and I kept retching. It even smelled green."

Jack looked up and grimaced. "Thanks for telling me," he said.

As Jack got to work on the smelliest person in the house, Susan said, "Your friends are at the door, Stevie. Now be careful out on that river. I know you've got proficiency certificates in canoeing, but the currents are bad. Wear the life jacket."

"Life preserver, and the scouts won't let you go on the water without one, sis. Don't worry, I won't get dragged down by the under *toad*." When Susan had been small she had misunderstood her parents' warning, "Be careful of the under tow," and used to have bad dreams about a giant toad waiting under the surface ready to drag children to a watery death.

Outside, the three friends mounted their cycles and rode to South Fambridge. South Fambridge, a small hamlet on the edge of the river Crouch, was where the scouts stored their canoes in a hut by the dyke. The journey took them about half an hour, through the villages of Canewdon and Ashingdon, but most of the ride was over flatlands and not difficult.

They each took a canoe and life preserver from the hut, plus splash decks and paddles. At low tide, there was very little river at all: just a sliver of silver in a cleft of mud. They had checked the tide tables for the month before setting out though, and sure enough the water was high up the banks. Had there been no dyke, the land around would have been flooded.

At the point where they put their canoes in the water, the river was about quarter of a mile wide. They did not intend to cross it, but to follow the south bank until they reached Brandy Hole, where they could enter the creeks and backwaters. On the river itself, there were speed boats, water skiers and motorized yachts. It was a crowded stretch of water, from Battlesbridge (the last navigable part of the river) to Burnham-on-Crouch (where it opened up into the sea) and they wanted peace and quiet.

They followed the dyke along, seeing nothing in the way of wild life but gulls, but when they turned into Brandy Hole, there were oyster catchers, avocets and all kinds of sandpipers, from knots to dunlin. There were also grey herons: solitary birds that rose from the reeds as gracefully as disturbed angels. Although Steve, Graham and Rosemary were not avid birdwatchers, these creatures were interesting enough, and made the canoeing worthwhile exercise.

The three were actually practising for a canoe race that took place every June from South Fambridge to Battlesbridge, a distance of some six miles. None of them had ever won it, though Graham had been a runner up on two occasions. The boy that had beaten him was three years older and would not be competing this year. So Graham was hot favourite.

"Okay," said Graham, his glasses tied on with elastic, "we'll use this stretch of water . . ." he

13

indicated a long channel between mudbanks dripping with bladder-wrack. Though the tide was high, the smell was still strong from the isolated islands of sludge, and the rotting timbers of old wrecks jutted aggressively from the higher mud like the bones of drowned giants.

They timed themselves, cruising, spurting and turning. Twice Steve went over and murky green water blocked his vision, but they had been taught to right the kayak-styled canoes by using the paddles under water. He emerged each time, dripping with salt water, his eyes stinging and his nostrils burning. Rosemary went over once, but Graham managed to avoid getting wet.

At one point Steve went off on his own to explore some twisting channels that worked their way inland. It was quiet and eerie, the banks overshadowing the canoe becoming very narrow at certain points. Steve saw a snake swimming alongside him and kept the paddle out of the water for a few minutes in case it decided to join him in his canoe. He was not fond of snakes: not as travelling companions. There were water rats too, but these bothered him less.

At one point, he was beyond the creeks and into brackish water. There were trees around him, and grasses that were not found out on the saltings. Suddenly, as he went beneath the shadow of an overhanging bush, the calm water spurted just in front of his canoe.

He jumped.

Then there was a pucking sound, on the canoe's waterline. Steve looked anxiously around him, wondering what was happening. Something was going on, but he wasn't sure what. All he could hear was the whisper of wind in the leaves of the trees and

14

the sound of his own paddles in the water.

Puck! Another pockmark appeared for an instant, on the surface in front. Small circles of ripples spread out from the spot.

The splash decks had prevented any water from getting inside the canoe, and from the waist down, Steve had been dry. However his feet began to feel damp now, and he realized that the canoe had sprung a leak. He would have to get back to the others – and fast.

At that moment, he saw a shadowy form among the bushes behind the dyke. The shadow moved, crouching low.

"I see you!" yelled Steve. "Who is it? What's the game?"

The figure rose out of the bushes. It was carrying a gun of some kind; probably an air rifle. Steve realized that the marks on the water had been pellets fired from this weapon.

The person carrying the gun was grinning. It was Gibbo Gibson. He must have followed them to South Fambridge. "Not s-s-scared, eh, Churchill? I could hear your teeth rattlin' from 'ere. Wassamatter, don't you like the ghosts of the creeks? They'll get you, you come up here. Nasty sods, drippin' green slime . . ."

"You shot a hole in my canoe!" shouted Steve, angry now.

The other boy levelled the rifle and said, "*Bang*! So what? What're you going to do about it, pal?"

Steve realized he was vulnerable. Gibbo could shoot holes in his canoe, or he could shoot holes in Steve himself. He doubted whether he would shoot at his body. Gibbo might not be frightened of Steve, but he was certainly scared of his own father, who used to beat him so severely that Gibbo had been known to limp for days afterwards. Steve might even have felt sorry for the other boy, if Gibbo didn't pick on him so much.

He knew something about Gibson which would help him gain some time. He began to paddle away, at the same time remarking, "You're not scared of ghosts, I suppose? You forget – your brother Ted told me you wouldn't go three times round the statue of the Viking in Hobblythick Lane, in case it jumped down and chopped your head off . . ."

Gibbo yelled, "That's a LIE!"

"Oh, yeah? Jimmy Hill," which was current street talk for pull the other one.

Steve didn't add that none of the boys or girls he knew would circle that statue. The local myth survived each new generation with as much strength as it had possessed in the early part of the nineteenth century.

"I'll do you . . ." and the youth with the air rifle swore violently, at the same time as trying to load his weapon.

Steve paddled furiously in the direction of the river and was soon around one of the channel bends of the creeks and out of sight of the marksman. He knew that Gibbo could not follow him over the mudbanks: they were far too soft, and the boy would sink, perhaps even disappear below the sludge. There had been many deaths in the creeks, especially hunters after the Brent geese that came down from Iceland in the winter months in their thousands. The men with the guns would get trapped by tides, or wander into quick sludge from which it was almost impossible to extricate oneself.

Steve found the other two still practising hard. "I've got a leak in my canoe," he told them. "I'll have to go back to the hut to repair it."

16

"How'd you manage that?" asked Graham.

"Must have been a bit of metal or something, sticking up from the bottom. It's only a small hole, but water's coming in. I'd better get back . . ."

"Okay," said Rosemary. "I'll come too. I want a drink."

"And me," Graham called.

They returned to the hut and they helped Steve get the now quite heavy canoe out of the water and empty it. Graham looked suspicious when he saw the small round hole on the waterline of the canoe, but he said nothing. The damage was soon repaired.

They went back into the creeks until the tide went out too far to allow them to continue their practising. Godwits came to peck at the exposed mud and crabs emerged from deep black holes in the banks to venture out in search of food. Seagulls flocked in, looking for soft-shelled creatures.

The three companions stayed on at the hut, using the scout cooking facilities to make themselves a meal. By the evening, the river and surrounding creeks had taken on a different aspect from that which they had enjoyed during the sunlit hours. There was a brooding atmosphere over the area of marshland. This was an isolated region of cold mists and voices amongst the reeds. The whole peninsula, incised by rivers and waterways – Thames, Crouch, Roach, Blackwater, Chelmer – had once been the haunt of Viking ships and in later years, smugglers. There had been deaths amongst those reeds, not only accidental, but deliberate. The sucking mud held secrets which would have shocked a world accustomed to violence. The slimeslicked ribs of wrecked craft were like curved prisons protecting outsiders from the horrors they contained.

17

It was a brave person that would walk the sea walls and dykes after darkness fell.

The three friends cycled home, reminding each other of the school expedition which was scheduled for Thursday and through the next weekend. They were being taken to Mount Kinder Scout, in Derbyshire by the PE teacher and some parents.

It was something worth looking forward to.

Chapter Three

Jack was driving Steve, Rosemary and Graham to the coach pick-up point outside Sweyn's School. Jack had switched on the radio and was singing along with a record. The other three were silent and gazing out of the windows. Two of their rucksacks were on the roof, the other was in the boot of the Mitsubishi Colt.

When the record had finished, Jack said, "Has any of you heard 'Piranha Love' by that new group, what'sitsname?"

Graham said, " 'FOLDing PLAStic'? They're not a new group, Jack. 'FOLDing PLAStic' have been going for years."

Steve could see Jack frowning in the rear view mirror and he squirmed inside with the embarrassment he knew his brother-in-law was feeling.

"Well, what is a new group? You tell me."

Rosemary replied. "The 'Ray Bees'."

Jack frowned again. " 'Ray Bees'? Never heard of them. What the . . . oh I get it – *rabies*." He was quiet for a minute, then he said, "That's not a very tasteful name for a group."

None of the others commented and, by the time Jack dropped them off, Steve was glad the journey had come to an end. It was always the same when Jack tried to get in on their scene. He always got it wrong. Rosemary said it didn't matter, that most adults tried and failed and no one thought any more about it, but Steve knew that it hurt Jack, to be thought a dunce when it came to pop music. He was only twenty-five after all, not fifty, but the music scene changed so fast you had to be teck to keep up with it. Even some of the kids at school were not breathing through the right tube when it came to it. You had to watch, listen and ingest every scrap of underground news on the latest groups to be teck.

The coach was in and waiting, since Jack had made them two minutes late, and they climbed aboard. They were going north, to Derbyshire and Kinder Scout. Steve was delighted that Gibbo Gibson was not one of the party, and doubly delighted that Julie Parker was included. Rosemary was sharing a two-person tent with Julie. He was sharings his tent with Graham.

The coach pulled out with twenty pupils on board, three teachers and three parents. They were soon on the Eastern Avenue and speeding towards the M25. Just before the motorway, Steve, who was next to the window, saw a grafitto on the side of a derelict house which read: I THOUGHT THE M25 WAS A NEW VITIMIN PILL UNTIL IT CAME THROUGH MY BACK GARDEN. He smiled at that.

One of the parents came to the back, to talk to them about the journey and their itinerary. Mr MacMasters had just returned to the area after spending four years with his family in Saudi Arabia. They knew all about him from his son, Jason, who had a deep tan and bragged about living in the Middle East, and how his dad was an "important oil man".

After he had gone over the same ground as their form teacher, Mr MacMasters said, "So who have we got here? I'd better get to know the names."

"Graham Chalmers," said Graham.

"Julia Stephanie Parker." Julie always gave her middle name, ever since seeing Stephanie Silva, in the film "Rag Dance".

"Rosemary Gordon."

"Ha!" said the adult, smiling. "Another expatriate Scot. I must get to know your family, Rosemary."

She did not tell Mr MacMasters that her grandfather had changed his surname to Gordon from a Dutch name that had been difficult for British people to pronounce. Rosemary's grandpa, though he spoke good English, had been fed up with having to spell his name out for people every time he said it. Even those that repeated it back to him destroyed all the Dutch inflexions and made it sound as if they had something stuck in the back of their throats . . . "Mr Jo Hhhraaarenegaahhh?" One day Old Man Jo went to the telephone directory, opened a page, and pointed to a word. It happened to be "Gordon" and thereafter this became the family name.

Mr MacMasters turned to Steve. "And you, young man? What's your name?"

"Steven."

"Steven what?"

"Winston." Steve turned back to watch the motorway traffic speeding past them on the fast lane.

"I think I know your parents," said Mr MacMasters. "Is your sister's name Susan?"

21

Steve nodded, his eyes still on the road.

Mr MacMasters was persistent, although he could obviously sense Steve's reluctance to communicate. The tone of voice he was using was as though Steve were an awkward child of ten. "And how are they? Your parents? I seem to remem—"

"They're dead," snapped Steve, cutting him short. He stared defiantly into Mr MacMasters' eyes. The man went red and looked confused at first, then embarrassed.

He mumbled, "I'm sorry," walked away to the front of the coach and sat next to one of the teachers. Steve saw him whisper to the teacher and then a few nods were exchanged. He felt angry. He was obviously the subject of that private conversation. To top it all, Rosemary said, "You didn't have to be so sharp with him, Steve. He was only asking."

"Well he won't ask again will he?"

Rosemary's eyes were on him. So were Julie Parker's: an hypnotic blue. Video eyes.

Rosemary said, "I don't understand you sometimes."

"Not much to understand. I don't like talking about – about my parents. They're dead and that's that."

He swung round and stared out of the window again, his eyes burning. Why wouldn't they leave him alone? Why did they always have to keep picking? Couldn't they see he wanted to forget about it. As far as he was concerned, he'd never *had* any parents.

They arrived at the camp site below Kinder Scout at about noon. After setting up the tents and making lunch, they went into Edale, to the Mountain Rescue Post for information packs. They told the officer in charge there just when they were going up Kinder

Scout, at what time and the number of people in their party – after all, better safe than sorry.

Mr Reit Johnson, whom all the kids called "Right", was the PE and Expedition master in charge of the party and he intended to follow the Pennine Way from Edale to Deepclough, going over Kinder Scout, Coldharbour Moor, and skirting Bleaklow and Shining Clough Moss. It was a good day's walk and he told them they would be starting off early the following morning. Right was not a tall man, but he was bole chested, with a deep voice. His broken nose, a badge he had acquired playing rugby, gave his square face an aggressive look. Indeed, the First Year were always told, on arrival at the senior school, that Right would sooner knuckle you in the kidneys than give you extra homework, or report you to your Department Head. The obedience he commanded was probably not so much due to this myth as to his broken nose. This awesome conk was always on display as proof that Right was not afraid to "mix it".

"I don't want anybody getting lost on Kinder," he said. "It's not high – only 636 metres – but it's awkward and full of bogs. We'll go down the other side to Snake's Road, across the Old Woman . . ." some boys sniggered, and Right glowered at them, silencing them immediately, ". . . which for the ignorant amongst us is a piece of physical geography, and not Arthur Daley's wife . . ."

"That's 'er indoors," muttered Steve, unwisely, and got a personal glare.

". . . and, if I can finish without any more interruptions, around Gathering Hill, over Wain Stones and past Torside Castle. I want you all to study your Ordnance Survey maps this evening. I trust you've provided yourselves with one each, not

23

one between two – if you get split up, you'll be the one without the map. So make sure you know the route. Ask a parent or teacher if you're not sure . . ."

He went on for another few minutes, and they all trooped back to the campsite. There was a visit to Castleton in the afternoon, and then a campfire in the evening.

Before Steve returned to his tent that night, he went up to Mr MacMasters and said, "I'm sorry if I was rude this morning."

The man shook his head fiercely. "No, don't worry Steven. I understand."

Something flared again inside Steve, and he wanted to shout. No, you don't. You *don't* understand. Instead, he joined Graham in the tent.

Graham was already in his sleeping bag and, as Steve was climbing into his own, the other boy said, "Steve, I've forgotten to bring my map. At least, I can't find it anywhere. Right'll kill me in the morning."

"Don't worry. You can share mine."

"But you heard what he said."

Steve snorted. "Nothin's going to happen. Have you see the size of that molehill outside? You couldn't get lost up there if you were blind. He's just doing what he's supposed to do – following the rules, whatever. We'll be okay."

Steve woke before the appointed six o'clock and went to the timber-built toilets to wash and clean his teeth. He met Julie Parker coming out of her side of the wash house and mumbled a good morning.

"Nice day," she said. "Is Graham up yet?"

Steve was conscious of his bare white chest. He draped a towel around his neck. "Still asleep," he said. "I'm just going to wake him."

Julie had her hair tied up in a pony tail, which swished as she turned away from him. "Okay, see you on the trail partner," she called.

"Yes – yeah – see you . . ."

He stood like stone for a few moments. She called had called him partner! His heart was still running full pelt around the edge of the campsite. Partner. Did that mean something? Was she just copying cowboy talk, because the Pennine Way was called a "trail", or did it mean something deeper? He shook his head to clear it of cotton wool. Better go and wake Graham.

They set off at six sharp, rucksacks on their backs, following Griod's Brook past The Neb, to the Fox Holes near the summit. It was not a difficult climb – certainly not a mountaineer's mountain – and could be accomplished by a grandmother in stout walking boots. The arduous nature of the ascent was in the pace set by Right Johnson. The PE master, and a couple of the parents, were determined to show that they were fitter than the youngsters.

Occasionally Right would look back and yell at the stragglers. "Come on! Keep up. This isn't a Sunday School outing." When they paused at all, he gave one of his little speeches. "We're here to work. Don't forget to look at the rock formations on your way, and notice how the brook has cut a deep channel in the peat. If you see any alpine flowers, or any plants you take a fancy to, *don't* pick them. Leave them to be enjoyed by others. Take photographs of the topography, not each other. We all know what you look like. Matthews, what are you staring at while I'm talking?"

"Bird, Right. Kestrel – look, up there."

"Good. Good powers of observation. Kestrel." A pause, then, "Are you sure it's a kestrel?"

Matthews shrugged. "Could be a goshawk. It's not a pigeon, anyway . . ."

They continued to the top, all the parents and teachers except Right panting and desperately trying not to show how tired they were getting. Some of the kids were beginning to wheeze too, but Right continued to forge a rapid pace. Steve knew that the PE master enjoyed destroying unfit parents and overweight teachers on these expeditions. He wasn't naturally vindictive. It was just his way of getting back at those who called him "musclebrain".

When they reached the plateau, Right allowed them all to rest, and Julie sat down next to Graham on a rock only big enough for the two of them. Steve and Rosemary had to stand. They broke open their Mars bars.

Graham said, "I bet Right would have given his left arm to be in the Falkland's war. He's a born yomper. Gimme the map, Steve. I want to see what sort of country this madman's going to yomp us over."

Steve handed over the map, and Graham adjusted his glasses before studying the terrain. "Just as I thought, Sergeant, we've got to yomp them up to the top of the hill, and yomp them down again."

They all began singing, "Oh, the Grand Old Duke of York, he had ten thousand men, he yomped them up to the top of the hill . . ."

Right looked across and gave them a grin. He was after bigger game than them, and they knew it. He wanted the other teachers and parents to ask for a respite: he wanted the adults to beg for mercy.

They started off again, along the path that crossed the moor. It was much colder now they were over two thousand feet up. Steve's breath came out in plumes in front of his face. His hands began to chill, as he held on to the straps of the rucksack which were now cutting into his shoulders. His feet felt like blocks.

Around them, in the heather, were sheep feeding on the sparse grasses of the peatland. It was essential to remain on the path, since there were ruts and holes in the black soft terrain, deeper than a man. Rocks jutted like giant fingers from the turf. It was a silent world, almost as eerie as the marshlands of the Essex coast, with its own spirits locked into the landscape.

Walking across Edale Moor, the plateau on top of Kinder Scout, gave Steve the feeling that he was on some prehistoric landscape; that there were creatures hiding from him in those black pits alongside the pathway. Strange smells wove themselves into his clothes and mists from the peat bogs slid across the damp ground like snakes, to wind themselves around his legs. "The monster from the Black Lagoon," he whispered to Rosemary, but she merely gave him a faint smile.

The cold wind dropped, which brought a slight relief to the party but, just before they reached Crowden Head, halfway across the moor, something serious happened.

A heavy mist descended. They had started the day in bright sunlight, down below, but the cloud base had lowered dramatically since the early morning. Within minutes it was like walking through a dense fog. Steve's clothes were dripping with water.

Right called a halt and asked everyone to gather round him. Steve shuffled forward with the rest of the kids to hear what he was saying. "I've got a rope here," he said, "which is long enough to accommodate all of us. I'm going to run it out as a line and I want everyone, *everyone*, to grip it with their right hands. I shall take the front and I want a parent – Mr MacMasters? Good, thank you – Mr MacMasters will take up the rear position. All those between the two of us must ensure that they don't let go of the rope and wander off the trail . . . can you all hear me?''

His voice was muffled in the mist, but there were calls of, "Yes – hold on to the rope.''

"Good. We don't want to lose anyone. Make no mistake about it, you can die up here, within a very short time. Even though it's spring down in the real world, up here it becomes very cold at night. You have a responsibility to me to keep that hand on the rope. We shan't be going at a fast pace any more. I have to find the trail and that's going to slow us up considerably. If you want to stop for any reason – an emergency toilet stop or something – yell out. I'm not a monster. I don't want any accidents of any kind. Okay? Right, let's get organized.''

The journey continued, with all the people in the party gripping the rope. Steve was almost at the end of the line. There was only Rosemary between him and Mr MacMasters. He could not see either of them, nor could he see Graham, in front. He felt alone.

About an hour after the mist had come down, someone, a boy, shouted that he needed to stop for a moment. The rope went slack in front of Steve and he let it fall for a minute to rub some warmth into his hands. Someone tried to push by him as he was doing so, and Steve stepped backwards, to let the person pass. His foot sank into some soft ground and then he felt himself sliding. His arms whirled as he tried to regain his footing, but he could not see the earth. He lost his balance altogether and fell through empty space. The fall was short. He had been on the edge of a bank about eight feet high. The impact, on hitting the bottom, knocked all the wind out him and, for a few minutes, he could not speak. He lay fighting for breath on the soggy ground, the thick mist like a blanket over his face.

As soon as he could, he sat up and listened. He could hear sounds on the bank above him. The others were preparing to move on. He tried to scramble up the bank, only to have the dark spongy peat come away in his hands. He fell backwards twice, before he realized he wasn't going to get up to the top without help.

He began yelling.

Silence.

"I'm here – down here," he shouted.

No answer.

They had gone on without him. He was trapped in a peat bowl with no one to assist him to the top. He didn't panic yet, but felt around the edge of the hole to try to find a gentler slope to climb. His legs sank up to the knees, and the black oily sludge sucked at his weight, trying to pull him under.

Chapter Four

Steve struggled in the sucking mire, pausing occasion- ally to yell at the top of his voice. Finally, he managed to tug himself out of the sludge using tufts of grass which he could feel but not see. By wriggling and pushing with his feet against the sides of the hole, he eventually reached what he believed to be the top. He pulled himself up and rested there. He was exhausted.

Lying amongst the wet, dripping heather, he took stock of his situation. The others had gone and, even if they now knew he was missing, they would be unlikely to return while the mist was still so thick. Right Johnson would probably wait until they got to the next Mountain Rescue Post, and leave it up to the professionals.

So, Steve was stuck. Even if the mist lifted, he had no map: Graham had held on to it after their halt at Fox Holes. He had a small compass, but it was a cheap one, and probably not very accurate.

Steve felt strangely calm. He was damp – wet

actually – and cold, but he didn't think he was about to die from exposure. But of course, it was early yet.

Feeling inside his pack, he discovered he still had two bars of chocolate left, an apple, a packet of biscuits and a tin of meat. The midday meal had been planned by Right, who had intended to stop at one o'clock to retrieve all the goods he had distributed amongst the hikers and cook it on camping Gaz stoves. Steve was not carrying a stove, but did have a box of matches.

Taking the matches out of his rucksack, he found they were still dry. He struck one and it flared, making the mist glow around him. There was no point trying to make a fire, everything was too wet, but he could have a piece of paper handy to make a brand. If he heard voices he could use it to direct them to where he was waiting.

He lay back on the mossy turf and stared into the mist.

After a period of time – he thought an hour at least – he looked at his watch. Only ten minutes had passed since he had crawled out of the hole! He couldn't believe it. He shook his watch, thinking that the battery must be running down.

Another hour turned out to be fifteen minutes, even though he left it twice as long before looking at his watch again. He groaned. "I'm going to be here for ever!" he shouted, petulantly, but his voice sounded hollow and quite unlike him. He was frightened back into silence.

After another undeterminable period of time had lapsed he took out his compass, struck a match, and tried to gauge the direction of North. It took seven matches. He twisted himself round until he faced South West. "If I start walking that way," he whispered to himself, "I should get to Fox Holes. Then I'll be able to find my way down the path by listening to the water running in Griod's Brook."

The warrior Thrang Noir, Steve's other self, would not have sat around waiting for something to happen. Thrang Noir was a do-er, not a defeatist.

He stood up, took a step, and almost fell down the hole he had climbed out of just a while ago. That's impossible, he thought, it should be behind me! If this way is South West, then surely the hole must be North East?

Steve took out the compass again, and checked it, using some more matches. He was right the first time, if the compass could be relied on, which it *had* to be, since he had nothing else to go by.

Cautiously, he worked his way around the edge of the hole, until he was sure he was on the other side. Then he took tentative steps forward, finding spongy ground underfoot. He wasn't on the path, that much was certain. The trail was on a firm ridge. Still, he had to trust to the compass, even though it was a cheap tin effort bought in a toyshop.

The going remained soft for some way and his progress was painfully slow. A chill was beginning to spread through his bones too, which was making him tired. Wet mist still clung irritatingly to his hair and dripped from his eyebrows; from his chin. Visibility was very poor.

At one point, a dark shape suddenly loomed above him. It appeared to have risen from the heather, inches from Steve's face, to tower over him. Bleak and menacing in form, it had a demon's flat features, with sunken pits for eyes. It stared back at Steve, unblinking, its mouth dripping saliva.

"Ahhh!" he yelled, loosing the breath from his lungs.

He stood, stock still with fright, for a moment, expecting the thing to move towards him. It stayed as frozen as he was himself, and only when he began to back off, did he realize what it might be. He crept forward again until he could touch its wet, slimy surface. It was a stack, a tall tower of rock that rose from the peat almost vertically. Steve laughed in relief, leaning against it.

Steve decided to have a piece of chocolate. He shrugged off the heavy backpack. On the rock ledge which he had taken to be a mouth, he opened his Cadbury's bar and broke off two squares. He put these in his mouth and let them melt, rather than chew them. The remainder of the bar went back into the pack.

For a while he remained by the rock, but since there was no wind it seemed silly to huddle beneath it and, readjusting his pack, he set off on his slow trek over the moor.

An hour later, Steve was back at the same rock. He stared up at it. The mists had cleared a little and he was able to see a few yards in front of his face. He would have missed the tower if they had been as dense as before.

He walked round the stone, thinking, it must be another one, similar, but not the same. He couldn't believe it was the *same* rock. His legs were almost dropping off, they were so tired. How could he walk so far and still not get anywhere? It was too bad.

Yet he knew it was the same rugged tower of gneiss that he had eaten his chocolate from, because, if he doubted it further, there was a sliver of silver paper from the bar still on the same small ledge. He stared at the stone in disgust, wanting to kick it to pieces. Wild thoughts were swirling around in his head now, and his shoulders were wracked with pain from carrying the pack. A headache was bothering him, just behind his eyes. It probably came from staring into the mist and seeing nothing.

"Bloody rock," he shouted, savagely, and his head rang with the shout.

Steve slid to the ground, his back against the tower. Taking the metal-foil survival blanket from his pack, he wrapped himself up tightly. He felt bitter with Right Johnson and the rest of the party. They had left him there. Did they even know he was missing yet? Why hadn't Rosemary said something? She must have felt the slackness in the rope. Why hadn't she told MacMasters that something felt wrong? None of them damn well cared, that's why! Graham was too interested in proving that he was the greater walker. And why had Julie Parker sat next to Graham at Fox Holes? Was his best friend secretly going out with the girl he was in love with?

"I bet they've been meeting each other," he told himself. "Going to the pictures. No wonder Graham's been telling me he's got to stay in to do his homework. Do his homework," snorted Steve, contemptuously. "He's been meeting Julie Parker on the sea wall, going for walks and things. Graham doesn't *want* me to be found." A sudden thought made him sit upright: I bet it was Graham that pushed me off the bank, into that hole!

After a while the bitterness abated and he was able to see that his argument had been unreasonable. For one thing he had never told Graham that he fancied Julie Parker, and for another he knew that Graham did his homework religiously, had always done so, because he wanted to join the Merchant Marines as a radio officer. That still left the query as to why Julie had sat next to Graham at Fox Holes, but that was hardly his best friend's fault.

"Even if she's chasing him," Steve told himself, "it doesn't mean he wants to go out with her. Graham's not interested in girls – never has been – he told me a couple of years ago that he'd rather be buried in lime up to his neck, salted and left for the crows, than go out with a girl."

Then again, two years ago Steve himself had felt the same way, but he had changed since then, hadn't he?

With these thoughts running through his head, he gradually drifted into an exhausted but shallow sleep, in which he was still aware of the chill that had control of his body.

Later, he awoke with a start, to find it was dark.

He felt stiff all over and the cold was eating through to his core. The metal foil blanket had slipped away and was now a crumpled heap around his thighs. He had great difficulty in standing and found he had to use the rock to pull himself upright, and even then he had to lean on it, to stay on his feet. He was numb in parts, wet and cold in others, and his teeth would not stop clattering. Movement did not help, and he realized he had to get some food inside him.

The tin of meat he had with him was useless. He had nothing to open it with. Instead he ate a bar of chocolate, some biscuits and the apple. It should have done him some good, though he didn't feel any different afterwards.

A wind sprang up. It cut right through him and the rock tower was not a great deal of help in offering resistance, since the wind screamed around its edges, finding him behind it. He had already put on the extra pullover he was carrying and the Kagool on top. He took his survival blanket and staggered away from the tower, looking for a depression. It was essential to get out of the wind.

Looking up, he could see the stars. The wind had chased away the mist and, hopefully, it would stay clear until tomorrow morning, when they came looking for him. As he moved through the darkness, he heard a sound ahead of him: a kind of snuffling. He stopped dead and listened.

"Hello!" he called after a while. "Who's there? Is anybody there? I'm . . . I'm over here."

Silence. Perhaps he had been hearing things?

He continued forward and, after a few moments, there were sounds of movement again.

"Hey!" cried Steve, angrily. "I know you're there. Why don't you say something?"

There was an answering snuffle. Something moved in the dark: a low, lumpy, stumbling shape. Steve's throat tightened. He could do without this. Perhaps there was a werewolf out there!

"I've got a gun! I'm prepared to shoot!" he cried, hoping werewolves understood English and knew enough about guns to be afraid of them.

"Baaaaa!" came the werewolf's reply.

It was then that Steve realized what was out there, in the darkness. Sheep! "A weresheep," he laughed, relieved.

He listened intently, the sheep would almost certainly have found shelter. He tried to locate their position, but his teeth were chattering so noisily that any further sounds the animals made were lost beneath his own.

Steve started to walk again and banged his shin on a rock. He moaned in pain. Now there was a sound quite near to him. Kneeling down in the soft wet heather, he felt around. There seemed to be a ring of waist-high stones, quite close together, and the sheep were inside this circle. He squeezed through, trying not to disturb the animals. At any other time they would probably have scampered away, but since they too were probably aware that it was warmer, if not safer inside the stone circle, they stayed.

Steve worked his way in between the docile creatures and lay, warm and comfortable for the next two hours, in their company.

In the early hours of the morning, just as the greyness was creeping over the moor, the sheep left him. Steve could not understand why they should want to go out into the wind again, but it appeared that they needed to eat more than they needed to stay warm. Steve remained in the stone circle, abandoned.

Since the ground was soft below him, he decided to dig a shallow hole which he intended lining with his survival blanket. It was best to do it while he was still relatively warm, since the wind was beginning to slice through him again. It whistled through the gaps in the standing stones, sharpening its cutting edge in the process.

He clawed away the peat in great lumps, soon reaching a depth of about forty centimetres. Then his hand struck something hard. It seemed to be a root or something, though there was not even a bush to be seen nearby. Despite his waning strength, Steve was curious, and pulled at the tuber.

It was indeed quite a thick black root which resisted Steve's efforts to pull it completely clear of the peat. It remained just clear of the ground. Caught in the tendrils at the exposed end however, was an object which took Steve's attention. He peeled away the tough root ends which were curled around the object like fingers, and eventually managed to wrench the thing from the root's grasp.

It was a knife! A crudely-fashioned dagger!

Steve knew almost as soon as the knife was in his hands that it was a weapon and not a tool: the blade came to a uniform point and both sides had been honed. This was not a knife made for slicing meat in a kitchen, or gutting fish, or for general outdoor use. This was a stabbing weapon.

Preserved by the peat, the blade was either very poor steel or iron. The metal had rusted but the cutting edges were still in evidence. There was a hilt guard, copper-green, and a tough wooden handle wrapped around with a material which appeared to be leather. At the top of the handle was a tight knot of wire. It was this part of the dagger that excited him most. The wire was made of a dull yellow metal which showed little signs of corrosion.

Steve was pretty sure that the knot was made of gold.

Just by the look and feel of the weapon, Steve guessed it was old – ancient. How old he had no idea, but it was not the kind of knife one would expect of a good ironsmith. It was a tribal weapon: a primitive's dagger. From his visits to museums Steve knew that even towards the end of the Dark Ages knives had been fashioned more skillfully than this particular blade. Of course, it could have been made by a shepherd, or a man too poor to buy a weapon manufactured by a professional ironsmith, but would such a man have the substance to decorate it with golden wire? Of course not.

No, everything about the dagger told Steve that he had found a treasure from the very distant past.

His fingers stiff with cold, but with a new fire of discovery Steve put the knife in his rucksack. He would show it to Right Johnson later.

That was assuming there would *be* a "later".

Steve stumbled out of the circle of stones, with the wind at his back. It was getting lighter all the time now and he was able to see his own footmarks. He was almost too weary to move another step.

Then he heard a shout.

"I'm over here!" he yelled. "Here!"

He saw them, moving along a ridge behind which the sun was rising. He was safe.

At first Steve felt like a hero. His friends had witnessed him being carried past the camp site by the Mountain Rescue Team and there had been awe in their faces. The doctor had now completed a physical examination and was asking him a lot of questions, many of which seemed irrelevant. Some of Steve's classmates were trying to get a glimpse of him through the window of the Rescue Post but Right Johnson's voice was calling them away.

"Can I give him a mug of tea?" asked Mr MacMasters, who seemed to have usurped a teacher's role and was the only school representative in the room.

The doctor nodded.

MacMasters passed him a steaming mug and Steve wrapped his fingers round it.

"Silly thing to do," said the adult, "getting lost like that."

"It would've been," retorted Steve, "if I'd done it on purpose. I was knocked over into a hole."

"Still . . ."

Steve looked away, angrily. Why did they always

have to do this? You broke your arm at rugby, or got cramp during swimming, and it was a "silly thing to do", as if you had done it deliberately. It wasn't as if he was even careless! He felt depressed now and wanted to go home. The adults in the Mountain Rescue Team had been great, joshing him, and treating him as if they had undergone a similar ordeal in their youth and knew how he was feeling; men with ropes slung over their shoulders and chinking metal equipment; men with broad grins, chapped hands, strong faces. They hadn't called him "silly".

"I suppose nothing ever happens to you?" muttered Steve.

MacMasters said, "What's that?"

"Nothing." Then a terrible thought occurred to Steve. "My sister . . . you didn't tell my sister?"

MacMaster looked surprised. "What? That you were missing? Of course we did, boy. Had to. Don't worry she's been told that you've been found. The moment they radioed down, I called her myself, both times."

You would, thought Steve.

Chapter Five

When Steve arrived at home, in the company of Right Johnson, he found Jack, Susan and Benjamin all waiting for him. Susan, white-faced, burst into tears the moment he entered the room and he was embarrassed as she hugged him to her in the presence of one of his school teachers.

"Sorry about all this," said Right, once Susan had released Steve. "We try to plan for every eventuality, but accidents . . ."

"We understand," said Jack, quickly.

Steve saw his sister stiffen, and he knew she was going to be critical of his PE teacher.

"Sis," he said, before she could open her mouth, "it wasn't anybody's fault . . ."

But Susan was not going to be silenced. "You should take more care of them," she said, starting to cry again; "your responsibility."

Right Johnson nodded, and Jack hurried him to the door, whispering something in his ear. Ben, on seeing his mother distressed, had started wailing too. Steve carried his rucksack upstairs to his room and undressed, climbing into bed without even bothering to wash. Then he remembered the dagger. He knew he should have said something to Right Johnson about the discovery but he wanted to hold on to it for a while. He would tell someone in the end. It was just that, well, it would go out of his possession once he told them and after all, *he* had found it. The weapon had lain in the peat for hundreds of years, so a few more weeks would make no difference. If he had not got lost, stumbled on the ring of stones and dug a shelter from the wind, it would not have been found. So, he felt entitled to keep it for a while.

Steve reached down and pulled the pack up on to the bed. He undid the laces and opened it up. The inside of the bag was soaking. The mist must have got into it while he had been on top of the mountain.

Steve took out the dagger and examined it in the light from his bedroom window. It was wonderful. Not so much magnificent or anything like that; it was not encrusted with jewels, or handworked with silver inlays. However, care had been taken over the golden knot that crowned the haft's butt. It resembled a turban woven from many yards of silk thread.

He put the dagger under his pillow just before Susan entered the room.

She sat on the edge of his bed. "How are you feeling?" she asked.

"Okay, now."

"Were you scared?"

He shrugged. "Not really. Not *scared* scared, if you know what I mean. Not like when a savage dog comes at you, or a truck just misses you in the road. I was worried some of the time, but I didn't believe I was in bad trouble. I didn't believe I was going to . . ." he stopped.

"Die?" she said. "You could have, easily. Anyway, you're home safe. I'm not going to let you go on another one of those trips."

"Come on Sue. You know it was an accident. It won't happen again in a million years."

"Mum and Dad were killed in an accident," she said. "I don't want – well, we seem kind of unlucky."

"But I'm here. Nothing did happen to me. So we can't be unlucky, can we? If I'd been killed – anyway, I wasn't. I'm okay."

"This time," she replied firmly. "That's why it mustn't happen again. You're not going on any more trips."

Jack was in the doorway.

"I don't think your dad would have put any restrictions on Steve because of one incident."

Susan snapped, "It's none of your business, Jack. They're not here. They went . . . went and left me with the responsibility."

"They didn't die on purpose Susan," replied Jack. "When are you going to . . ."

"If they had any thought for us, they wouldn't have been speeding along the motorway at eighty miles an hour. They were careless, Jack. I don't intend to be as selfish."

Jack put his hand on her shoulder. "Sue, Sue, think what you're saying. You and Steve, well, you talk as if your parents went out intending to leave you forever. When you talk about them, that is. You're so bitter, the pair of you. Good heavens, people drive at eighty on the motorway all the time. They were unfortunate, that's all. Wherever they are now, they're . . ."

"They're nowhere," snapped Steve, his eyes on Jack's face. "They've gone, and that's that."

"Don't you believe in an afterlife?"

"I don't belive in anything like that. There's nothing there. Is there Sue?"

His sister looked about to cry again, but she seemed to fight down the tears. "Enough talk," she said, tucking him in fiercely. "You need some rest. Jack, go and take care of Ben. You've left him alone down there."

Jack shook his head slowly and then left the room.

"Now, sleep young man. I'll be up later with something to eat, but you look exhausted."

She left him and he fell back on the pillow, gratefully.

"You've got a visitor."

Susan was in his room again, but he had woken up refreshed and almost ready to leave his bed. He had been promised some food on a tray – fried potatoes, egg and bacon – and he did not want such a treat to escape him.

Steve guessed it was Graham or Rosemary. Though he himself had been driven down from Derbyshire by hired car, the others were following on shortly afterwards in the coach. They would be back by now. "Okay," he smiled, "send 'em up. You all right now?"

Susan nodded, her eyes clear.

A few moments later the doorway was filled with radiance as a figure stood there, bathed in the sunlight from the window. She had a box of chocolates in her hand.

Steve sat bolt upright in bed and breathed the name: "Julie!"

Julia Stephanie Parker glided into the room looking

a little shy. As an only child it was doubtful she had been in a single man's bedroom before, and Steve was conscious of the fact that he still had his vest on. He wished he had remembered to put on some snazzy pajamas, if he had owned any snazzy pajamas, which he didn't. Thank God he hadn't put on his faded blue ones, with red and yellow lorries all over them! He went into a cold sweat at the thought. At least a vest was slightly macho, wasn't it? It would have been better to have been bare chested, except that his chest wasn't fit to be seen before it had been taken on its annual holiday to Spain. Even then, compared with Graham's, it was like the flatlands of Essex as opposed to the Rocky Mountains. Still, a vest was pretty naff.

"Hello," said Julie in her Stephanie voice, "are you feeling any better?"

"Yes thanks, much better." He felt as if he ought to cough or something, to reward her for her sympathy.

"I just brought you these," she handed him the chocolates. "I'm not sure whether you're supposed to eat chocolate after such an ordeal."

She said the word "ordeal" as though it were decorated with curlicues and flourishes.

"Everyone's proud of you," she continued, when he did not answer. "A bit of a Robinson Crusoe on the quiet? Mr MacMasters said you did all the right things to keep from getting exposure. He's very knowledgeable about such things, isn't he?"

Steve felt a stinging reply coming to the end of his tongue but he forced it back down his throat, where it lodged.

"Well," she sighed, her dress swishing as she walked towards the door, "you're obviously very tired. I'll see you later."

"Yes, right . . ." Now was the time to ask her for a date. All he had to say was, "When? How about the pictures tomorrow?" but he hesitated. What if she curled her lip in revulsion and looked on him as if he were a reptile? What if she said: "I'd rather go out with Quasimodo." It was one thing to visit a sick classmate; quite another to go out on a date with the possibility of being kissed by a youth with a concave chest and a gnat bite on his nose. (No, wait, the gnat bite had gone . . .)

"Graham's taking me to look at the river," she said. "He's nice, isn't he? Well, cheerio. See you at school, probably," and then she was gone.

NICE? Graham was a roach; a flea-infested river rat with two faces; a stinking slug dragging its slimy body over the Essex landscape; a pig with a snout the size of two cannons; a gungy slob. "I *knew* it," Steve muttered into his pillow. "That rat's been seeing her behind my back. Well I hope they're both happy. I hate the pair of them. They can rot for all I care."

Later, Rosemary called to see him.

"Hello Rosemary, you look nice. What have you done to your hair?" said Steve.

Rosemary regarded him with suspicion, her round face going dark for a moment. "Hair? It's the same as always. What's the matter with you?"

"Nothing. I was just thinking how nice you are."

"I think I'll go home," she said. "I don't like the look of that sickly smile on your face. Did you get bashed on the head when you were lost?"

Steve became huffy. "No, I didn't get bashed on the head."

"Well, snap out of it boy."

Graham was right behind her. Steve felt his heart harden and his eyes turning to flints.

"Wotcha mate," said Graham, sitting on the bed with little grace or thought for what lay beneath the blankets. "Got any of those chocolates left?" His muscular arm reached out for the box.

"Buy your own damn chocolates," said Steve, snatching them out of his reach. "*You* can have one," he said sweetly, to Rosemary.

Then to Graham, he said, "How was your walk?"

"What walk?" Graham took a chocolate, ignoring Steve's efforts to keep them out of his way. He popped it into his mouth. "What walk?" he repeated.

"The one you had with Julie Parker," said Steve in a silky voice.

His friend shrugged. "All right. Why? She wanted to see the boats. Funny girl that – bit touchy." He took another chocolate.

"You mean sensitive?" said Rosemary.

"I mean touchy. She keeps touching you when she talks to you – touching your arm and that."

"Really?" said Steve, stiffly.

"That's because she fancies you Gray," said Rosemary, in a matter of fact voice.

The youth looked incredulous. "Get out. She doesn't fancy *me*. She talks about Gibbo Gibson all the time."

"Well, you and Gibson. She talks about both of you."

Steve coughed. "Does she – does she ever talk about *me*?"

Rosemary screwed her face up in deep concentration and remained that way for at least a minute, then she said quite simply, "Nope."

"Oh, well that's a relief," cried Steve. "I wouldn't

want her getting touchy with *me*."

"You're safe," said Rosemary.

"Good."

There was silence in the room after that – silence except for the sound of Graham crunching or squashing chocolates in his mouth. Steve felt under his pillow. The sheet and the pillow were sodden. That was strange. The knife was still there, though. He took it out.

"How about this then?"

Graham and Rosemary stared. "What is it?" asked the girl.

"It's a dagger. Found it on top of Kinder Scout while I was lost. Looks old, doesn't it?"

She took the knife and felt it. Then Graham did the same.

"How old do you reckon?" said Graham.

"Dunno. See that," he pointed to the knot, "that's got to be gold – precious metal – otherwise it would have rusted, like the blade and the bit at the bottom of the handle. Look, you can polish it . . ." he rubbed it against the sheet. "See?"

Rosemary looked impressed. "Gold? You mean it's an ancient dagger? This is an antique, a relic – you're not supposed to keep thing like this."

He snatched it back. "Don't be such a wimp. Anyway, I'm not going to keep it forever. I just want to hold on to it for a bit, get used to it. Once I get bored with it I'll hand it over to someone."

"And they'll ask you why you didn't do that in the first place."

"So what? What are they going to do to me? Shoot me? There's too many rules and regulations in this country. It's time someone made a stand. Just because Maggie Thatcher says no, slapped wrist

48

Rosemary, you do everything you're told."

She lifted her nose. "No I don't. Keep the grotty thing. You obviously see yourself as some kind of rebel without a cause. Come back Jimmy Dean, Jimmy Dean – all is forgiven."

"What do you think, Gray?"

Graham shrugged. "Country's not going to fall apart if you hang on to it for a bit, is it? You could get some sort of reward when you hand it in. Don't you get a quarter of it's value or something? I saw a programme once about treasure hunters. They got the stuff from wrecks – dived for it. Silver ingots, stuff like that."

"What's the rules about finding things on mountains?" asked Steve. "National Trust, isn't it? Don't the government own the land? I bet they don't give me anything. They'll whip it away without a thank you. I want to get some photos of it first. Get my picture in the local rag. Then they can have it, once I've had a bit of glory."

Graham used his John Wayne voice. "So you wanna be famous, kid? If ah had ma druthers, I'd druther be rich."

They left him then. Susan had come up the stairs with the meal she had promised. He ate it and then spent a restless night, having slept all day.

Outside, over the creeks, the moon tossed the clouds around. He stared out of the window, at the sea wall, trying to imagine Julie walking along it, through the waving grasses, beckoning him. "It's not Graham I came to see," her whisper would float up to him. "It's you. You Steve. I only got to know Graham so that I could see you. He's nothing to me. I was just shy, that's all. And Gibbo Gibson . . ."

Steve's heart hardened a little and the dream evaporated. Rosemary had said that Julie Parker also fancied Gibbo Gibson. Any girl who could fancy Gibbo Gibson must be touched in the head, as well as touchy with her hands. If she thought Gibson was the end of all things, then she deserved to be barred from membership of the human race.

Water dripped from the windowsill where the dagger lay.

Water again? The dagger must be hollow, thought Steve. It must be filled with peat-bog water. He reached out and touched the weapon. It felt so frozen it almost stuck to his fingers. Steve stared at it. Something strange there. Something out of the ordinary. It gave him a peculiar sensation in his stomach.

He left it where it was and tried to get to sleep. Once or twice he got up to look out of the window again. Ever since he had been back from Kinder, he had had the strange feeling that the house was being watched by someone: that *he* was being watched.

Chapter Six

When God made the world he never got around to finishing one corner of Essex. He fiddled with with a few marshes and quagmires, but the evolution he encouraged elsewhere somehow got forgotten in Paglesham. Things were still crawling around in the primeval swamps of that confluence of estuaries when Jack and Susan bought the terraced cottage which used to be part of the old Trading Post. They liked the idea of having misty prehistoric flatlands on their doorstep. In the winter, the winds came directly from Siberia, but in the summer they had to put up with offensive odours.

When Steve threw open his bedroom window to allow entry to a stream of air, it was accompanied by the stench of creekwater mud. He hoped it would chase away the smell of damp wood.

Jack was half walking, half running along the unmade road, his bowl of cornflakes spilling over as he spooned them into his mouth. Whopper, coming the other way, stepped aside and leaned on his blackthorn stick. The old smuggler watched Jack hurry by and he shook his head. Once Jack was round the corner Whopper continued his journey towards the creek. When he was below Steve's window, he stopped and looked up. "If ever they decides to have a cornflake race in they Olympics, we got oursens a gold medal in your Jack," he said. "I reckon he'm the best runnin' scoffer on two legs."

"You're right there, Whopper – hey, wait a minute. I've got something I want to ask you."

Whopper was always ready to pass the time of day with anyone especially the young, who he said were closer to his "method of thinking" than "fully growed" adults. "I'm a-waitin'," he said, the crooked blackthorn walking stick which he had made himself bending under his weight.

Steve grabbed the dagger from behind the curtain on the windowsill and rushed downstairs with it. Susan was in the kitchen, so he got out of the front door without her seeing him. Whopper was waiting in the road.

Steve showed the old man his prize. "Look, I found this up in Derbyshire. Any idea how old it is Whopper? You've seen some things in your time. Have you ever seen a knife like this?"

Whopper hitched up his baggy trousers around the top of which a piece of baling cord served as a belt. He stared at the item, cocking his head to one side. Finally, he said, "Nope, can't say I 'ave. Where'd you say you found 'er?"

"Derbyshire, on the top of Kinder Scout – that's a mountain."

"Foreign, eh?" Even though Whopper had travelled all over the world in his younger years, he still liked to play the village yokel. Anywhere outside Essex he called "foreign".

His gnarled and seamy hand, weathered by a thousand saltspray storms and arctic winds, reached out to touch the knife. The second those fingers touched the haft of the weapon, they were withdrawn quickly. Whopper said, "I don't like they."

Steve was shocked and puzzled by Whopper's reaction. He had never seen anything bother the old smuggler before. Steve had seen him plunge his hands into the steaming entrails of a freshly killed rabbit, and not even flinch. Yet here he was, worried by an old knife. "What's the matter with it?" he asked.

Whopper wagged his huge cauliflower nose. "I don't know, I don't know. I don't like the feel of 'er. 'Er's too froze to my way of thinkin'. Not your natural cold, neither. I don't like 'er." And with this uncharacteristic reaction, he clumped off along the lane, forgetting even to say goodbye.

An unnatural cold? What did that mean? Steve had to admit the dagger did have an unusual temperature about it – it *did* seem very cold to the touch – but he put that down to the fact that it had been locked in peat for many hundreds of years.

He shrugged. Whopper was a funny old boy anyway. He wouldn't even go to Canewdon village, just two miles away, because he said it was full of witches . . . "*Allus be witches there booy, until they church tower falls, so they says. Six of 'em. Three in silk, an' three in cotton, so they story goes. That's three rich 'uns and three poor, to my way of thinkin'.*"

Once back indoors, Steve put the dagger in the back of the sideboard in the living room, behind some of Jack's papers. Then he went into the kitchen, to say cheerio to his sister.

Graham was sauntering along the road and they joined up to walk to the bus. Rosemary was standing on the corner, yawning.

As they climbed aboard the bus, Gibbo sneered at Steve. "Did the little boy get lost then? Churchill lose his way up the mountain?"

Steve had had enough of Gibson. "You shut your mouth," he said.

The other boy stood up. "Yeah?" his face looked savage and Steve's courage failed him for the moment. He remained silent, hurriedly pushing past Gibbo while still attempting to retain some honour.

"I'll see you later," snarled the other boy, his fists knotted. Steve knew that if he had been in range he would have got one of those fists in his back. Gibson was no coward, but he had no scruples either. He would hit you anywhere: front, side or back, above or below the belt. He would kick you when you fell, too. However, Gibbo could also dive from the top of the mill into the river, a height which sent eels slithering down the spines of other boys and girls. He could climb trees and swing from one top branch to another. He could do tricks on a BMX or skateboard which would have other kids gnawing their tongues in envy, too frightened to try the same acrobatics themselves. Steve had to admit that if you put Gibbo's spirit in Graham's body you would have an English village Rambo.

"You get right up my dad's bugle," shouted Gibson, and some of the First Years on the bus laughed at this inane witticism. It made Gibson happy. Gibbo was tough, thought Steve, but he was also pretty thick.

The rest of the day went without any untoward incident. Steve was treated by the teachers and the other kids with a certain amount of deference. He was famous among his classmates for a while. He did his lessons as usual, enthusiastic over those he enjoyed, and working on those he did not. It was his intention to get reasonable if not good GCSE passes. He didn't know what he wanted to do with them, but if he could not be as strong as Graham, or as tough as Gibbo, he was going to show that he had a brain worth holding in his head. Rosemary helped him a lot, since most academic subjects seemed to fall naturally into her hands.

"I don't know how you do it," he said to her. "Doesn't seem fair. I sweated blood over that essay on Ted Hughes' poem and you hardly looked at it at all. You get an "A" and I get a "B+". It just doesn't seem fair."

"Fair the boy wants? He tries to match a MENSA girl and almost makes it through sheer grit and determination, and *still* he's not satisfied."

"MENSA? That club for eggheads? You don't belong to MENSA."

She tapped her temple. "No, but I've got the wherewithall, sunshine. I have an IQ that would make your toes curl to hear the figure. I just don't believe in joining clubs or secret societies."

He snorted, impressed by her confidence. "What is it?"

But she just smiled her round-faced smile, and refused to divulge the mysterious figure.

On the bus going home that night, Gibbo seemed to have forgotten the morning's incident. He sat just in front of Steve and, halfway home, turned round to put a few questions to Steve regarding his ordeal on the mountain. Gibbo spoke in a sort of casual way, as if he wasn't *really* interested but saw no harm in asking. Steve found it difficult talking to the other boy as if there were no hostility between them, but he did his best to keep the strain out of his voice. He was relieved when Gibbo turned back to his friends. Steve wasn't sure he liked Gibbo's friendly interest in his activities any more than he did his animosity. It was difficult to choose between them.

When he entered the house he went straight to his room to get his homework out of the way. He called to Susan that he was home and that he didn't want to be disturbed.

"No comics . . ." she shouted, having once caught him reading *Asterix the Gaul* when he should have been doing homework. Under his bed was a small pile of precious comics: *Judge Dredd*, *Violent Cases*, *Swamp Thing*, *2000AD* and two classics, *Dr Faustus* and *King Oedipus*. These were relatively expensive comic books, the artwork being exceptional. Their value was not understood by Jack or Susan whose childhood comics had not gone beyond *The Dandy*, *The Beano* and the American pulp comics like *Superman* and *The Hulk*. They did not understand that modern illustrated comic books were now designed to attract an intelligent adult readership . . .

". . . and no Dungeons and Dragons, Mr Loup!" came Susan's warning, clearly an afterthought to cover all possible distractions.

"I'm *trying* to do my homework," he yelled back, indignantly, "and I can't get it done with all these interruptions. Anyway, it's Graham who's The Wolf. I'm Thrang Noir, Black . . ."

"Get on with it."

There was quiet after that.

By the time he had finished his homework, Jack had arrived home and dinner was ready. Steve closed his books and went downstairs to indulge in a banter session with Jack. Unlike most parents, Jack was close enough to Steve's age to be able to give as good as he got when it came to mickey-taking, his dry wit almost always defeating the youngster in the end.

They had dinner and then Steve went down the darkening lane to Graham's parents' bungalow, close to the dyke. Steve stood briefly on top of the dyke and saw that the tide was coming in: the yachts and boats had their bows pointing down river. Steel cable stays tapped away at hollow alloy masts filling the air with the sound of tubular bells. With fifty different-sized craft bobbing around, subject to eddies, currents and breezes, the notes were many and varied. To one unused to this weird continuous symphony of Aeolian bells such "music" might be eerie, but the hollow tones were somehow comforting to Steve, who had been raised within their sounds.

Shadows crept across the water: sinister shadows with vaporous bridal trains. Suddenly the whole scene took on a different aspect. There were frowns on the surface of the river as the wind rose a little in strength and in the marshes on the other side unseen shapes were moving amongst the reeds. Dark thunderclouds rolled over the horizon and Steve sensed someone's presence. The watcher was out there.

Steve left quickly, running down to the bungalow. Graham opened the door and shouted, "It's only Steve," to his parents, somewhere in the depths of the home. The two boys then went into Graham's bedroom where he kept his computer. He had a new game called "Excalibur" at which neither of them were yet proficient, which meant that it was still fun. They each took a control stick and battled on the screen, knight against knight, the animated figures in bright colours dying, recovering, dying, recovering, as if there were no end to a violent life, only a fight that went on forever.

Later, when Steve arrived back at his own house, he found Jack in a bit of temper. "What's wrong?" he asked.

Jack was crouched at the living-room sideboard with a bucket and sponge. Susan was standing over him. Steve noticed the dagger had been placed on the coffee table, along with some very soggy looking papers.

"I don't understand it," muttered Jack. "There's no pipes behind here? Where did the water came from?"

Susan turned to Steve. "Just after dinner we heard something dripping. There was water coming from the sideboard, running under the doors. You didn't do anything, did you?"

"Of course not!" he said, indignantly. "What would I do? Throw a bucket of water in there?"

Susan said, "No need to get upset. I'm only asking. You could have knocked over a vase of flowers or something."

"What flowers?" Jack said, emerging. "There weren't any flowers on the sideboard. And Ben has been in bed for ages. I just don't understand it. There's got to be some sort of explanation." He looked up at the ceiling and shook his head. "Can't see where it came from."

"Condensation?" suggested Steve, helpfully.

Jack shook his head again. "Not that much water. Look at my papers, they're ruined."

"We'll peg them out on a line in the bathroom," said Susan. "I'll get them dry for you."

"Yes, but they'll be all crinkled. I'll get hell from the bank. And there's our own stuff in amongst my work papers – insurance certificates, all that sort of thing. Is that yours?" With the last sentence Jack pointed to the dagger and the question was directed at Steve.

"Yes – yes Jack. I found it."

"Rusty piece of junk. Don't put it in the sideboard. Put it outside in the shed. It's stained a couple of my papers."

Steve could not believe he was getting off so lightly. He had expected intense questioning.

"Yes Jack, sorry."

Susan said, "Where did you get it? It looks like a knife."

"On that school trip, to Kinder. I found it on the moor. Didn't look worth handing in or anything."

"Looks like it's fit for the dustbin," said Susan, turning away.

It was obvious to Steve that both Jack and Susan had given the dagger only a cursory inspection and they thought it was something someone had thrown away. He picked it up and took it out to the shed at the bottom of the garden.

The night had descended. Steve felt around in the garden shed for the shelf where the hedge clippers and other small tools were kept. He placed the dagger amongst these. Then he stood, looking through the shed window. Something moved across the pane and a scrabbling sound made Steve jump.

"What's that?" he cried, stepping back on a tool that fell over and clattered to the shed floor.

The scratching sound came again and the shed door began flapping in the wind, banging. Something darted across the window pane a second time.

"This is crazy," muttered Steve. His heart was pounding in his chest.

He turned from the window and went outside, locking the door behind him. As he made ready for a dash to the house, he peered around the corner of the shed. In the darkness he could see one of the branches from the willow tree blowing backwards and forwards, brushing against the window pane. Finding out what was the cause of the movement and noise should have made him feel better, but it didn't. He still felt uneasy. There was a prickling sensation at the back of his neck.

"Crazy," he repeated.

He decided not to dash back to the house, because that would allow the panic in him to run wild. Instead, he took a slow stroll along the winding path, between the willow and the silver birch. The light in the front-room window was reassuring. Nothing could jump out of the darkness and sink its hideous teeth into his throat whilst that light was on. It was a link with normality. Demons didn't like ordinary, everyday things that brought comfort to their victims. They had to wait until people stank with fear and all worldly things were out of sight and mind.

Steve shouted, "I'm just coming in." He tried to keep the panic out of his voice, but it sounded taut and strained.

He opened the door and entered.

Jack looked up from sorting out his wet papers. "What?"

"I – I just said I was coming in."

"What for?" asked the exasperated man.

Steve shrugged. "I didn't want to frighten Susan. She might not have seen me go out."

"Oh," said Jack, accepting this explanation only

because he was preoccupied with other troubles. Susan look quizzically at Steve.

"Are you all right? You look a bit pale."

"I'm fine – fine. I'm off to bed. See you in the morning."

He climbed the steep stairs, had quick wash and brush of his teeth, then jumped into bed. He tried to bury his fear in thoughts of school work and games.

Outside, it had begun to rain.

Chapter Seven

Steve woke suddenly to the sound of heavy rain beating against the window panes. He felt terribly cold, as if he had been locked in a freezer for some time. It was not the coldness of winter winds, nor even of snow and ice, but the zero temperature of a place beyond this world.

He sat up and blew on his hands, trying to get some feeling into them. Dreaming. He had been dreaming of something, or somewhere, beyond now, beyond here. None of the images remained in his head, but there was an aftertaste lingering in his conscious, of a land of terrible misfortunes. Perhaps he had read a comic lately, which had failed to register properly in his waking mind, but which he recalled in his sleep? That was possible.

Steve rubbed his feet back and forth on the bedclothes, hoping the friction would warm them. The window panes still rattled with the rain. It seemed to come in sweeps and gusts, drumming one minute, and tapping the next. It was not a night to be out and Steve hoped that Whopper, who slept on a dirty old tub moored near the oyster beds, was not suffering too much. Steve had been on the hulk where Whopper stayed when he was not in The Plough and Sail, and he knew it to be rotten throughout. The craft, which was not even a houseboat but an old cockle boat, leaked both from above and below. It was a wonder that Whopper had not caught pneumonia before now.

Steve switched on his bedside lamp and stared up at the window. The swirling, whirlwind night hammered at the loosened panes, trying to squeeze between them. He could see the raindrops smacking against the window, running down as bright drops in the lamplight. From outside came the sound of wind crashing in the trees and the creaking of branches rubbing against boughs. Somewhere in the night a creature was shrieking: a fox or a squirrel. A bin clattered in the distance. Steve felt very uneasy, restless. He certainly could not go back to sleep and, for some reason, the room seemed forbidding.

Perhaps Steve should go and see if Whopper was all right? The old smuggler's pride was such that he would never knock on a door, even if he knew he was on his last legs. It wouldn't take much to put on his Kagool and run down to the wharf.

Careful not to wake Susan or Jack, Steve got up and dressed in warm clothes. Gradually the heat was coming back into his bones, into his limbs, though deep inside he still felt chilled. It was a strange business. He sat for a few moments, one sock on and one in hand, trying to remember his dream. Perhaps when you had a nightmare, your mind commanded your body to react to the temperature of the place in your dream? Psycho-something, it was called. After all, Steve told himself, the mind was in the brain and the brain told the rest of you what was happening. So if the brain thought it was freezing, then it would tell the body, "Listen chum, it's taters outside, so why are you still warm?" and the body would cool down accordingly. Psycho*somatic*, that was it; old Bankcroft's lesson on interaction between mind and body. If you thought you were ill (even when you weren't) and got obsessed by it, you sometime made yourself ill. Maybe it was the same with temperatures?

He crept down the stairs and took his Kagool out of the cupboard underneath, then made his way to the door. Perhaps he should make a flask of tea to take with him? It sounded a good idea, but the noise would surely wake the others. Steve decided against it and opened the back door, leaving it unlocked.

Once outside he wondered whether he was doing the right thing. The rain was coming down in rods, driving into the ground. Although his waterproofs kept him dry underneath, Steve did not feel he could be out in it long. He sploshed through deep puddles in the unmade road and found the footpath which led by the cornfield to the part of the river where Whopper's boat was moored.

Although it was dark Steve was familiar enough with his surroundings to find his way to the river without any problems. However, journeys through darkness and rain always take longer than normal, and he found himself battling against wind and water merely to reach the dyke, a quarter of a mile away. Hedges reared up as he was passing them and it would not have surprised him if they were torn from their roots by morning. A distant roll of thunder had him worrying about lightning for a moment, but since it seemed so far away he dismissed his fears.

The rain was noisy against his hood, deafening him to all but the loudest sounds. His eyes began stinging under the continuous bombardment of raindrops. Soon he was regretting ever leaving his bed and venturing out into the night.

When he got to the dyke, he had difficulty in climbing it in his wet slippery wellingtons, but eventually he got to the top. The rain had lessened in intensity however, and had dropped to a fast drizzle. A faint dawn lit the edge of the horizon.

The river was raging, sending long reptilian tongues of water out to lick at the boats on its surface. Under the sky, always awesomely big in the flatlands, the fields were gradually emerging. The sea of reeds out in the dengies had been swept flat against the bog.

By the time Steve got to Whopper's ancient cockle boat, the rain was down to a fine Irish quality and he felt a little foolish in coming out. Still, he called to the old man:

"Whopper, you all right?"

There was no answer from the dank dark craft.

"Whopper? It's me, Steve."

He stood there a long time after that, and was just preparing to go away, when a figure emerged from the rickety wheelhouse. It was Whooper in vest and pants. He had something in his hand: a gun of sorts, though it looked both unwieldy and useless. Steve remembered that the old man kept it to scare away unwelcome visitors.

"It's me, Steve. Steve Winston."

The gun was lowered.

"What'dyou want, booy? You'll catch you death o' cold out 'ere on a night like this."

"Came to see if you were all right. There – there was a storm."

"You get on home. I'm all right. I don't know what they folks of yours is thinkin' of, sendin' you out 'ere."

"They don't know. I didn't tell them I was coming. I just got worried about you, that's all."

Steve was close to tears for some reason. Whopper was right. Why *had* he come out? There had been worse nights when he had not even considered Whopper. There were also more than a dozen men, mostly old sailors, out in the dengies on similar half-submerged craft. Had Steve ever thought of them? No. No, there was another reason for coming out to see Whopper. It was to get away from the house. Somewhere in the back of Steve's brain was a fear of his own room, and he did not know why.

"Go on home, booy. Ol' Whopper's big enough to look after hisself. I thank you kindly," he added, as he stared at Steve's face.

"That's okay," mumbled Steve, and he turned and walked back along the top of the dyke to the footpath.

As Steve walked home, a thought came into his head which he had been trying not to consider since the evening before. *The water in the sideboard*; where *had* it come from? It seemed that wherever the dagger was placed became wet. Steve could not blame it on a hollow handle any longer; there had been too much water for that.

When Steve reached the house, the drizzle was still coming down through the murky light. At first he headed towards the back door, but a movement in the front garden attracted his attention. There was a noise: an irregular banging. Perhaps Jack had woken up, found him missing and was out looking for him?

66

"In trouble again," murmured Steve to himself. "Might as well face the music now."

He took the path around to the front of the house and, as he turned the corner, a prickle of apprehension raised the hairs on the back of his neck. Someone was in the front garden, but it wasn't Jack.

The shed door was open and swinging in the wind. Occasionally it banged shut, then flew open again. Steve strained his eyes to see through the fine drifting rain and swirling greyness. The willow near the shed partially obscured it, but Steve could just make out a shape between the flapping door and the window.

"Hello?" he called.

He was frightened now. If it wasn't Jack in the front garden – and the figure was too short for his brother-in-law – then who was it? Perhaps he should call Jack?

For some reason, he didn't, though his fright did not diminish. He just stood there and gazed, trying to make out who or what stood behind that drooping screen of willow branches. The leafy curtain swayed this way and that in the wind, but never did it reveal the shape behind it in full. All Steve caught were some swift glimpses. He could have gone indoors, called Jack and left it to the man of the house, but his feet wouldn't move. It was as if they were fastened to the floor, stuck in frozen mud.

A cock crowed and made Steve jump.

Finally, he was able to move his legs, but they took him round, in front of the shed. Dirty shadows were chasing each other over the lawn. There were open patches appearing between the dark clouds, sending mouldy shafts of light slanting down.

He saw something which made his throat constrict. Within the drizzle that drifted down from the sky was an area of tightly compressed rain, as heavy as the earlier deluge. It seemed to have formed itself from the lighter mizzle around it: a dense figure of raindrops. Steve had no time to study this dark shape of rain, before it was driven hard by a sudden gust of wind against the side of the shed. Large globules of water splattered against the panes of the window, and ran down the creosoted woodwork, forming an oily pool at the bottom. A sudden breath of winter filled his lungs. Steve shivered violently, the bolt of terror stunning him like cold electricity. He felt he had been touched by a chill not found this side of death.

A cry caught in the back of his throat like a trapped bird. The incident had rocked him. He felt as if he had witnessed a shocking event, as if someone angry with the world had thrown themselves away like a basin of waste water. All that he had witnessed was a shadow, darting sideways, but it *felt* like more than that. Steve's whole body was still tingling, uncomfortably, with the shock.

He looked around for an explanation to this phenomenon. Perhaps the shadow of an overflying heron? Or even a plane? Instinctively he reached out for natural reasons, clutching at them to save himself. Maybe all he had seen was a freak patch of rain caught in the circle of hanging willow wands? Pressure? These strange occurrences were often due to pockets of low pressure, and the light – the light was unusual. Twilight was a time for quick-moving shadows and trickery. In the dawn things darted back and forth without seeming to move. Steve often tried to catch them, unawares, but they flitted by at the corners of his eyes.

The willow branches rustled, shedding droplets of water, as if the tree had straightened and shaken itself. Again, something reached out and touched him, chilling his bones. Steve stepped backwards, startled by his own fear.

At last he found his voice. "GO AWAY!" he shouted.

Now, a feeling of great sorrow filled Steve's heart; an ancient melancholy almost too terrible to bear. Something dark moved within the willow wands. Heavy drops of rain again struck the window with the sound of sleet driving against a metal panel. They rang notes out of those panes and the tones were mournful.

Steve shuddered involuntarily. He stared at the place where the dark rain had been, trying to convince himself that it was a hallucination. Yet, he had *felt* it, not just seen it. He went over to where the oily pool lay. He kicked at it with his boots. It splashed like ordinary water. Then he looked up, saw an object through the shed window.

The dagger.

"What are you doing out there?"

Steve jumped at least three inches off the ground. Then he recognized it as Jack's voice, coming from the house.

"Your sister will have a fit if she sees you. It's only five-thirty."

Steve ran to the front door where his brother-in-law stood in a dressing gown. "I – I thought I saw someone – in the front garden."

Jack looked concerned. "What, now?"

"Yes – but when I got out there . . ."

"Okay, but you'd better get up to bed, before Sue wakes."

Steve nodded. "Yes Jack."

He did as he was told, leaving Jack staring out into

the oncoming murky day, no doubt searching for Steve's mysterious visitor. Steve was too weary and confused to describe what he had seen, and he suspected that Jack would poohoo such talk. Stripping off his wet clothes, he put them where Susan would not find them, and climbed the stairs in his vest and underpants.

When he got to his room he found that the "thing" had been there, while he was out. There was a wet patch on the carpet by his bed.

Still shaking, he climbed beneath the sheets. Within minutes he had fallen into a fitful sleep. Although he was asleep, he was aware of being so. His dreams were cold. He was back in the frozen land again.

Someone was on his bed. He could feel the weight. Fearfully, Steve opened his eyes, and through a kind of misty haze he recognized his sister. He sat up.

"Sis?"

"You were calling out. I thought you were having a nightmare."

"I – I was. I dreamed of this – this ghost made of water."

Susan smiled. "I know. It's all right now, anyway. I get bad dreams too."

"You see rain ghosts?" said Steve, hopefully.

"No, I dream . . ." she hesitated, then continued, ". . . I dream of – of Mum and Dad sometimes."

Steve frowned. "Bad dreams?"

"Well, not very nice ones. I mean, I'm angry with them. I shout at them for . . ." she stopped there, and looked away.

"For leaving us?" Steve said.

She turned and looked at him sharply now. For a

moment he thought she was annoyed with him, then she nodded, slowly. "I suppose you're right, though I hadn't thought of it that way. Still, it's no good – they're not going to come back are they?"

"They can't," said Steve. "They're dead."

Susan nodded again. "Your dreams, Steve. The ghosts – they aren't Mum and Dad?"

"I don't think so." He wanted to talk about something else now, but Susan would not leave the subject alone.

"We've never really spoken about them, have we? Not since the accident. I suppose that's my fault. I found it – difficult. Still do. For some reason this – this unreasonable anger erupts inside me, every time I think about them. Silly really, because they couldn't help it. I don't suppose they *wanted* to die. It's not as if they committed suicide or anything . . . I don't know. Listen Stevie, they were good to us, when they were alive. A little selfish I suppose, but they were young, with lives of their own. I remember as a young girl thinking how nice it was to have young parents."

"I know, I know, I remember them too. I wasn't born yesterday."

"No, of course not, but maybe I've – perhaps I'm responsible for your view of them now."

"My view? Oh, you mean why we don't talk about them? Well, you said they were going too fast in the car . . ."

"That's what the newspaper said: 'exceeding the speed limit'. They were doing . . . oh, I don't know, Dad always was a fast driver and people were always warning him that he'd come to grief one day. Jack wouldn't ride with him. Mum never said anything, never told him off for it, just sat in the passenger seat and never murmured. I supposed if she had ever put her foot down – put her foot down – that's funny. It was him that put *his* foot down."

They both laughed, and then Steve felt a flush of shame for giggling over someone who was dead; who had died in tragic circumstances. "I dunno," he said, "I just get angry."

"You get angry too?"

He nodded. "I want to punch someone. I want to punch Dad. Do you think that's crazy?"

She patted his hand. "No, I don't."

Suddenly, she looked concerned and put her hand over his. He tried to withdraw, but she held on to him.

"You're cold," she said, "you're freezing. What's the matter with you? Do you feel ill?"

He shook his head. "Just cold."

"Shall I call the doctor? That doesn't feel natural."

"No. I'm all right, honest. I was – I was just dreaming about the North Pole. It's psychosomatic."

"It's *what*?"

Steve grinned. "I'm not saying it again. It was hard enough the first time. Next time it'll come out 'somopsychatic' or something."

"But what does it mean?"

"It means I only think I'm cold. I'm getting up. I'll be down in a minute. A hot cup of tea will do me good."

"Well, I hope so." She left him then, but not before glancing at the walls of his room and saying, "It's a wonder you don't have nightmares about motorbikes."

He stared out at the day. The grey was swirling away into the clouds. Some bright patches were showing. Now that Susan had left him alone and the numbness of sleep had worn off, he felt the scared, sick feeling return to his stomach.

He needed to talk to Graham and Rosemary.

Chapter Eight

As he dressed, Steve was still in a terrible state.

One half of his mind told him that ghosts did not exist, that there was nothing after death, not even Heaven and Hell. His parents had proved that. He felt sure he would know if they still existed, even just in spirit, wherever they were. He would *feel* it.

The other half told him he had seen something out in the garden, in the rain, early that morning. He had seen it and felt its presence. It had reached out and touched him. Even as he pulled on his clothes his stomach turned over with the fear the memory induced in him.

Steve stumbled down to breakfast. Benjamin, secured by a harness, was standing in his high chair and raining puffed wheat like manna on the floor beneath.

"Ya!" he yelled, his little mouth breaking into a gummy two-toothed smile when he saw Steve, but although Steve was usually charmed by Ben's obvious affection for him, he was too distraught this morning. He gave the baby a half-hearted grin.

Benjamin, disappointed that he was not going to get thrown up and down, or be allowed to sit on Steve's shoulders and pull his uncle's hair like a horse's mane, assumed his pharaoh pose again and returned to the business of distributing grain to the masses.

Susan said, "Steve – are you sure you're all right?"

"I'm okay," he said, wearily sitting down. Ordinarily he would have liked to stay home to catch up on his sleep, but he had to talk to his friends. Also, it was his sister's day out in town, shopping, and he would have been left alone in the house. That thought alone was enough to send a trickle of ice water down his spine.

"Just a little tired," he added, when he saw she was still staring at him. "Honest. I'll be fine, sis."

He glanced at the window. "Is it – is it still raining?"

Susan opened the back door and peered out. "No, it's stopped now, but you'd better take your water-proofs. I'll get them for you."

"NO!" he said sharply, remembering they were still soaking wet and that questions would ensue. "No, it's all right. I'll get them." He jumped up from the table and went past her.

It wasn't raining. He was safe, for the moment.

Somehow he got through classes that day and after school he suggested to Graham and Rosemary that they all vacate the bus at the turn-off to Paglesham and walk the rest of the way home. It was a three-mile trek around country roads and along footpaths.

"I've got something to talk about – important. I don't want to chat on the bus in front of Gibbo and everyone else."

74

Rosemary and Graham shrugged at each other and then agreed. Strolling home from the corner was something they did occasionally, but not while the skies were black and rain was threatening.

"We might get wet," said Graham, still unsure, as they jumped from the bus and started along the country lane.

"We'll be okay," said Steve, absently. He could see Gibson staring at them.

They set off beside the deep ditch that followed the road.

"Well?" said Rosemary, after a few minutes. "What's the problem, Steve?"

"Yeah," lisped Graham, hitching an imaginary shoulder holster, "come on blue-eyes. Tell ole Bogey what you can't tell the Feds."

Steve was quiet for a while. Even though the other two were his best friends, he still wasn't sure they wouldn't laugh at him. However, he felt he had to have advice and he did not know who else to turn to. "Do you believe in ghosts?" he blurted out.

Rosemary glanced at him, while Graham seemed not to have heard.

"Ghosts?"

"Yes, you know – ghosts. Things that go bump in the night."

"I believe in spirits," she said, "so I suppose that's the same thing. I mean, I don't think we just die and disappear . . ."

"I've seen a ghost," he said, turning on her so quickly that she backed away a little. "Last night." He turned to Graham, "Last night," he repeated.

Graham looked at him steadily, then with a curl to his lip said, "For crying out loud. You're not serious?"

"I'm telling you . . ." said Steve.

But Graham stamped off in disgust, saying angrily, "Bloody loony."

Steve had expected his friend might laugh but he hadn't guessed he would get upset.

Rosemary put her hand on Steve's arm and whispered, "Gray doesn't like to talk about ghosts. Let him go on ahead on his own. He gets nightmares."

Steve laughed, hollowly. "He gets nightmares. *I* get the real thing."

Rosemary was looking into Steve's face and he wondered if she belived him. "I saw this ghost," he mumbled. "I did see it. You'll probably say it was a dream or something, but I know it wasn't. You know these things, because you can feel them. As soon as I saw it, I knew it was a ghost. Maybe even before I saw it, because I've had this funny feeling ever since we came back from Kinder, like I'm being watched. I thought maybe it was the shock – you know – the doc said I might feel a bit strange for a while, because of the exposure and being lost. I thought it was that. Anyway, it's hanging around our house. It wants something from me, but I don't know what to do."

He was shaking a little at the end of this speech and he knew from Rosemary's expression that she believed he had seen something.

"Perhaps – perhaps it wasn't a *real* ghost," she said, "but something the shock brought on – a hallucination . . ."

"I thought of that," he said, hopefully.

". . . but in any case, it's real to you, isn't it? I expect you're anxious to do something about it before you go crazy. I know I would be."

He wanted to hug her for understanding.

Instead he explained about the previous night's happenings, gesturing wildly sometimes, and his voice cracking at others. He hadn't even realized how frightened he was himself until it came spilling out.

Rosemary's round face looked serious as she pursed her lips. "So, you think the ghost was after the dagger?"

"Had to be. Nothing like this ever happened before I found that thing, and he – *it* – was staring at the knife, trying to get at it. It leaves wet patches all over the house, wherever the dagger is, and sometimes it comes to my room. I don't know what to do. Why doesn't it take the thing if it wants it?"

Rosemary appeared to be concentrating, then she said, "Because it can't. It can't pick it up, otherwise it would have done. Why is it so important? That's what we have to find out, then we'll know what to do with it."

Steve stopped and stared at the lowering sky. "How are we going to do that?" he asked, bitterly. "I mean, you can't ask it questions. It's made of water."

Rosemary hooked her arm in his, in a chummy fashion. "Listen buddy, you can find out *anything* from books. So long as you know what you're looking for. Let's see what we've got . . ."

Graham was about a hundred metres in front as they turned off on to the footpath which ran between Paglesham Churchend, and Paglesham Eastend where they lived. Several fields separated the two parts of the village.

". . . we know it's got something to do with the dagger and something to do with rain."

"Not much to go on, is it?" said Steve, gloomily.

"Cheer up, Steve. We'll exorcise this ghost for you." She gave his arm a squeeze. "Leave it to me.

Call round my house later this evening. Okay?"

They parted then. Graham was already entering his garden. He gave them both a kind of apologetic wave, and Rosemary returned it.

"You mustn't mind about Gray," she said. "He's got a thing about ghosts. With me, it's snakes."

"With me it's Gibson," muttered Steve, seeing the farm boy sauntering along the river levee in the distance.

Steve went directly to the garden shed and found the dagger. He left his school books on the floor of the shed and ran down to the dyke. The tide was out and the mud creeks were exposed all the way over to the sea, some five miles distant. He intended ridding himself of the dagger and, hopefully, the ghosts, for good. If it wanted the knife then it would have to dig around in the mud looking for it.

Steve drew back his arm and threw the dagger out into the slick alluvium. It turned over and over in the air, before descending. He saw it splat into the mire about a hundred yards from the dyke. It sank immediately. He remained on the dyke and stared at the small hole the weapon had made on the grey surface of the sludge. While he stood there it began to drizzle with rain.

"That's that!" he said.

"That's *what*?" came a sneering voice from behind him.

Gibbo.

Steve turned. "Gibson, leave me alone. I've got no time for messing around here with you."

"Time you was taught a lesson," said Gibson.

"If you like," answered Steve. "I haven't forgotten you holed my canoe with that air rifle. I'm fed up with you Gibson, calling me Churchill, and making remarks. You might beat me in a fight, but I'm fed up with you." This was true. He didn't care whether he got hurt. It was a way of taking his mind off insubstantial things like ghosts and getting rid of his feelings of frustration and helplessness.

Gibson came forward, swinging his arms. He hit Steve two or three times on the chest and shoulders, while Steve managed a couple back. Both boys stepped away from each other after this initial testing foray, then just as Gibson looked about to come in again, his eyes widened and his face lost its colour. Steve moved forward to hit his opponent but stopped when he saw that Gibson was frozen to the spot.

Steve felt as if a cold wind were blowing on his back. He began turning slowly, into the slanting rain. Like the Ancient Mariner, he knew that there was something terrible standing right behind him.

Then, before he was fully round, he stopped. He didn't want to see it. He knew it was there, could feel it, and the horror of its presence was plain enough in Gibbo's eyes. The bully's mouth was now open in a scream, but no sound was coming out. It was as if the scream were on a frequency too high for human ears; a note that Gibbo could not bring down, because his terror was at the same pitch.

Gibson's eyes were bugging, and suddenly his scream came down to the level of the human ear. It came out as a raw whistle from his throat. The youth turned and ran off, slipping over several times on the wet muddy ground. He didn't look back.

Steve copied the other boy, except that he was too weary to run, and went at a fast walk. All the way home he sensed that the phantom was just behind him, keeping pace, but not once did he dare to look back. He knew it was there, and that in itself was enough to fill him with a fear that he had never known. That alone was enough to crowd his head with images he had never seen.

The terrified youth reached his house and went inside, going straight to his room. He looked out of his window into the garden below. Something was under the weeping willow, the suggestion of a manshape, screened partially by the hanging wands. Then Jack came along the path, head down, looking preoccupied. He was carrying his briefcase and an empty cereal bowl. He apparently did not see the shadowy form under the tree, passing it without even a glance.

Later, when it had stopped raining, Steve ran around to Rosemary's house. "It came again," he told her as she let him in. "Gibbo saw it. The rain ghost scared him off. Ask him if you don't believe me."

She gave him one of her characteristic stares and then said, "Of course I believe you. Anyone who saw your face at this moment couldn't help it. Buck up. We'll get rid of it."

She led Steve through the living room, past her parents. He said good evening to them and received a smile from Rosemary's mother and a grunt from her father.

They went up to Rosemary's room. Graham was sitting on her bed when they entered and Steve felt mildly betrayed.

"You said . . ." he began, but Rosemary interrupted him.

"I had to get Gray in on it. I didn't have the right books. I went round his house and we linked the computer to a library information mainframe."

"Call me Hotwire," said Graham.

"Anyway," continued Rosemary, "we've got something."

Graham muttered, "I know what we've got. We've got a phone bill that my parents will go spare about." He explained to Steve. "We had to use the phone line to hook into a computer memory bank in London. The phone bill alone'll cost a fortune, and that's on top of the bill for using the IBM."

"Thanks Gray," said Steve, humbly.

Graham shrugged, then got to his feet. "I'm going. I don't want to know about all this spooky stuff. I've got enough to worry about. My father's going to chop my head off while my mother watches, knitting her cardigans. Oh well. Is it still raining out?"

"No," said Steve, "so you're all right. The ghost only comes in the rain and then it hangs around my garden mostly."

"I *really* don't want to know," Graham muttered, shuddering. "I'm getting home before it's dark."

He left them. Steve heard Rosemary's father grumble something about "Piccadilly Circus" as Graham went through the living room again. Then he turned to Rosemary. "What've we got then?"

Rosemary threw herself on to her bed and opened a notebook which had been lying on her pillow.

"First, I tried myths and legends, but though there were a few possibilities there, it seemed to me that the spirit that's haunting you must have a historical background, mustn't it? After all, the dagger's real. So I asked the computer about people living in the area of Kinder Scout, that had anything to do with water. I thought maybe we would come up with some tribe that worshipped rivers or lakes. We got zilch.

"Then Gray suggested rain. I'd never heard of rain

worshippers but we gave it a try. Bingo! It came up with an ancient tribe called the Regn-rinc, or Warriors of the Rain. These people had a terrible battle with a rival tribe, the Warriors of the Sun, who drove the Regn-rinc out of their valley and up on to a plateau, where many of them died from their wounds.''

"The top of Kinder Scout!" cried Steve, excitedly.

"Exactly. An iron age tribe chased up the mountain and slaughtered there.''

Steve nodded, impatiently. "But why does he want his dagger back? I mean, he's dead now. What use is it to him?''

Rosemary said, "I'm coming out of that. Listen. 'When the warrior died, they were buried with all their worldly possessions, including their weapons. They would need their amulets and cloaks, their swords and spears, in the Otherworld, beyond death.' ''

"Was it their Heaven, or what?''

Rosemary looked up from her notes. "It was both Heaven and Hell. They only had one place which dead warriors could go – that was Ifurin.''

"So why is the dagger so important?''

Rosemary pursed her lips. "We had to break the connection with the mainframe. We never got that far. Maybe it's his treasure? You know, like the pharaohs got buried with their gold and jewels?''

"Maybe. I dunno. I threw the dagger in the mud anyway.''

"Steve, you didn't!''

"I thought it would get rid of him.''

Outside, the evening was calm and relatively dry. Steve made his way back to his own house, his brain in a less settled state than the weather. He had to think about what Rosemary had told him. He wasn't sure what it all meant. The weapon was still there and the spirit of the warrior knew where it lay. What was the difference between the knife lying in the mud, and lying in the peat on top of Kinder Scout? It was all a bit confusing. Maybe the rain ghost was just punishing him for taking the weapon in the first place? Perhaps now that it had frightened him a couple of times it would go away, return to this Ifurin place?

As he passed the shed, he glanced quickly at the willow. There were no dark shapes hiding behind the screen of leafy branches. He let out a sigh of relief. He was so tired he knew he would drop off the moment his head hit the pillow.

Just before he fell asleep an hour later, a thought came into his head. A horrible thought. The root on the moor that had been gripping the dagger – the gnarled root with its knobbly tendrils from which Steve had prised the weapon – that root wasn't a root at all. That root was the mummified arm of a corpse! Those tendrils were the corpse's fingers! Not only had the peat preserved the weapon, it had preserved the warrior's body too. Steve had peeled away the dead man's fingers and wrenched the weapon from the petrified hand.

Chapter Nine

Steve's eyelids felt as if they were sealed together. He forced them open and gradually took in the scene around him.

He was lying beneath a leafless tree. Around him was a barren rocky landscape covered in hoar frost, over the surface of which roamed slow-moving mists. The light source seemed to come from above, but it was a hazy diffused light, that fell evenly over the whole place. Somehow he knew there was no sun above that bland sky. The whole world was the colour of Jack's pewter beer mug, with little variation in shade.

Steve touched the frozen trunk of the tree and found it was made of stone, the branches formed of roughly-hewn chunks of rock, jointed in many places. It was as if someone who liked trees had stuck pieces of stone together to remind them of what they missed.

He climbed to his feet and shook the frost from the

animal-skin cloak which was barely keeping him warm. It was then he noticed the two other humps on the ground. Shaking Graham first, and then Rosemary, he said, "Time to move."

Graham sat up, stretched and yawned. Then he blinked and looked around him. "Where are we?" he said.

"We're in the Deadworld," Steve answered, and he wondered how he knew.

"Lost souls," Rosemary said. "Lost in Ifurin."

She climbed to her feet and surveyed the landscape. In the distance Steve could see mounds rising out of the white mists. Rosemary was looking towards the mountains. "We have to go that way," she announced, her slim hand pointing from beneath her cloak.

Graham said, "Are you sure?"

Rosemary replied, scathingly, "How can I be *sure*? It's a guess, but it's based on what I feel to be right. We have no real way of knowing which path to take – it's a matter of making a choice based on instinct."

The other two did not argue with her. In her character role as L'épervier she had a high orientation factor, which meant on excellent sense of direction. Certainly Steve, a charismatic warrior, would not have known back from front, and although Graham's orientation was higher than his own, the muscular youth had never come near Rosemary's ability for finding a way through a maze. They each had particular skills and relied on one another in different kinds of emergencies and for a variety of decisions.

Graham took off his glasses and wiped the fog from the lenses. "Let's get going then, but you'd better be right Rosemary."

They set off across the crackling, icy wastes, their

breath coming out in plumes. Steve's muscles felt tight and weary at first, but the brisk pace soon loosened them. The windless plain around the trio seemed full of menace. Steve knew it was important to keep his wits about him at all times, no matter how much the cold dulled his thinking. The cold seemed to come up from the ground – a metallic chill – and bit deeply into his bones.

Bleak rugged scenery stretched over a forever landscape broken only by the shrouded mountains.

Suddenly three figures sprung from behind a tor. Dwarflike and horrible, they barred the way; snarling. Thick arms sprouted from powerful shoulders; wild hairy heads shook with rage as they formed a wall of muscle across the path.

"Me!" said Graham, divesting himself of his cloak. He leaped forward and grappled with the middle dwarf, wrestling the creature to the ground. The other two jumped on him and for a few moments there was a frantic struggle which sent hoar frost showering over the two watchers. Steve put his hand beneath his cloak and found the dagger. He let it rest there for a moment. Graham was not in any serious danger. This was merely a harassment, or perhaps a distraction. It was best to keep back and watch the landscape for other attackers: to be ready in case a more deadly foe came crashing over the plain. Steve was under no illusions about his mortality: he could be killed in this place, if he relaxed his vigilance, or failed in combat with one of its monsters.

One of the dwarves went flying through the air and crashed on the ground hard with permafrost in the shadow of the tor. It did not rise. A second dwarf let out a yell and, jumping up, limped away into the mists.

The third dwarf was on its feet instantly and Graham was only a split second behind. The pair of them stood facing each other. The dwarf was blowing noisily, out of breath. It made one last mad rush at Graham, who swept it aside, sending it tumbling head over heels. When it regained its feet, it too ran off into the mist, shouting curses and promising that, should there ever be a rematch, the youth would be sorry.

Rosemary tended Le Loup's wounds, and the three companions continued their journey through Ifurin.

They came to a sluggish river, full of snow slush and impossible to swim. Muscles would have seized before they reached the far bank.

"There's a bridge further down," said Rosemary, "we'll have to take our chances crossing it."

They reached the bridge, a strange structure which appeared to be fashioned from the rotting timbers of ancient ships; the wood black and sodden. Beams and planks were tied together with gangrenous sail ropes, the knots complicated and impossibly tight. Though there was no wind, the bridge creaked and moaned. They tested its strength. It seemed that the pulpy planks would hold only one at a time.

The far side of the bridge was locked in fog and they could not see the bank. Rosemary went across first. She returned, out of the mists, a few moments later.

"There's a giant, an ogre, guarding the other side," she said. "I couldn't get past."

Steve took out his dagger. "It has to be me, this time," he said, gathering his courage.

The giant was waiting for him: taller and more shaggy than a Scots pine, its strong-looking limbs twisted and gnarled. It let out a roar as Steve approached, its mouth opening to reveal a cavern. Steve attacked without waiting for the giant to come forward.

The youth wielded the weapon with great skill, his reactions sharpened by a thousand video games. Steve feinted, and weaved, in and out of the giant's blows, he had fought such fights on Graham's computer many times before, and he allowed his instinct to rule each swift move.

Then the unthinkable happened. Steve was knocked sideways by a random blow and dropped the dagger. A huge foot came down on his back and pinned his body to the earth. Steve felt one of his ribs crack. Frantically he clawed the ground, trying to locate the dagger. He was useless without it.

If this is a dream, thought Steve, *I shall not wake up*.

Suddenly his scrabbling fingers touched a hard object. They closed quickly around the dagger. Steve swung his arm, stabbing at the giant's instep. The knife sank into flesh. The foot was gone. Steve was back on his feet, despite his painful chest.

Another bellow, this time one of rage.

The ogre, furious at this failure, crooned at the pewter sky, its face darkening and its eyes burning red. Steve taunted his opponent, knowing that its temper would defeat it, would spur it to a hasty, wrong move. Clumsily, the giant swiped the air about the youth's head and stamped the ground causing the landscape to tremble, only to find the youth had anticipated and skipped aside.

Finally, Thrang Noir slipped up under the giant's clutches and stabbed the fiend behind its knee, cutting the hamstring. The ogre let out a roar of pain, staggered sideways and fell crashing into the icy river. It disappeared beneath the slush.

Steve called the other two and they crossed the precarious bridge one after the other to join him.

After a long arduous journey over the frozen wastelands they reached the mountains and the three caves, one of which led to the world outside, the real world, beyond Ifurin.

Rosemary suggested the middle cave and they travelled through passageways full of wraiths and orcs, Steve having to use his dagger in numerous battles. At each fork Rosemary was required to choose a path, and did so with care. Only once did she make a near-fatal mistake.

Finally, they came to the end of the passageway. The exit was guarded by an enormous dog. It seemed they were going to have to handle this monster together, if they were to reach the outside world.

They fell upon the creature.

Graham, with his high strength potential, wrapped his arms around the throat of the beast. The spiked collar pierced his arms, but he continued to strangle the terrible creature.

Rosemary tried to distract the hellhound by somersaulting over its muzzle and yelling oaths.

Steve rushed forward and attempted to pierce the brute's heart with his dagger. As the blade sank in, the creature twisted its head sharply, divested itself of Graham, and closed its jaws on Steve's head. In another second it would have crushed his skull. Rosemary rushed forward, throwing her shoulder behind the hand with the dagger, forcing the knife into the beast's chest. The hellhound screamed . . .

Steve sat bolt upright with a cry.

For a moment he stared wildly around him, wondering where he was, and then recognized the familiar items in his bedroom. He rubbed himself through his pyjamas, working some warmth into his limbs.

"Dream," he said, hoarsely. "Bad dream."

He swung his legs out of bed and as his feet touched the floor he felt the dampness. The rain ghost had been again while he was asleep. He looked out of the window. It was a wet world but the rain had stopped.

Safe for the moment.

It was six o'clock in the morning. He dressed hurriedly and then ran down to the river, climbing on to the levee. The tide was almost out. Somewhere in the mud was the dagger. Steve knew now that he had to get the knife back and return it to its rightful owner. He didn't even want to think how the latter could be done, but the first thing was to retrieve the blade, *if* he could.

He took off his shoes and socks and began to walk out on the mud. Within seconds he had sunk to his knees. There was no way he could reach the spot where the knife lay. He turned back to the dyke, the frustration building in his chest. Whopper was standing, leaning on his blackthorn, by Steve's clothes.

"Want to go out on the mud, eh?"

"Yes," said Steve, distractedly.

"Want that knife en chucked in t'other day?"

Steve looked up at the old man. "How did you know?"

Whopper chuckled, revealing tobacco-stained teeth. "Seen en lob 'er out there. Know where 'er is too. Know this bog like the back of me 'and. You'm won't get out there a-walkin', booy."

Steve sighed, staring at the slimy greyness between him and his goal. "I know that."

"So, what we'm need is old-fashioned dustbin lids," laughed the smuggler. "They'm got those black plastic bags these days – they'm no good. Metal dustbin lids is what we want."

"What for?"

"What for? Why, for wearin' as shoes, that's what for, booy. Like them there snow shoes they'm Eskimo fellas wear. Stops 'em from sinkin'."

Steve's heart lifted. "Really?" Then it sank again. "Yes, but where are we going to get dustbin lids from?"

"I got a set," said Whopper. "Use 'em to go out to the middle, like now when tide's on the ebb. Just a small stream there then and all the fish is concentrate in a yard wide o' water."

"Can I borrow them?" cried Steve, jumping to his feet.

Whopper scratched his hoary grizzled chin, and shook his head once, in a characteristic gesture. It looked like there was a big problem. "Borrey? I don't know they word, booy. I heard of *hire* that word I'm familiar with – but *borrey*. Nope, that's not a word as is in my vocal list."

"Fifty pence," said Steve, used to Whopper's haggling.

"I was thinkin' more on a pound."

"Done," Steve shook the calloused hand. "Pay you Tuesday."

"Not now?"

"You know the rules, Whopper. I can only draw out my pocket money on Tuesday. I've got none of this week's left."

Steve's parents had left him some money – not a lot but enough to allow him some spending – but Susan would only let him have it once a week and then only three pounds. He would have liked a paper round but there were none available out in the country. In the summer holidays he worked in the fields, pea or potato picking, but the rest of the time he relied on his trust fund.

Whopper got the dustbin lids, slightly bent and sadly rusted in places, from the rotting hulk he called his home. Then from the dyke and with the aid of his stick, he guided Steve over the mud of the dengies.

"Go on, go on," was accompanied by a wave of the blackthorn.

Steve, his legs apart to splitting, splodged forward, step by step over the soft mud. Around him seagulls carked, apparently disliking this invasion of their territory. Out in the middle, a thin dribble of saliva, the river trickled. Terns skimmed over its surface and dived occasionally.

Eventually Steve got to an area where Whopper shouted for him to begin searching. Left to himself, Steve would have looked further over, towards the moored yachts, now resting upright on their twin keels. However, he trusted Whopper's judgement.

He felt around amongst a sludge full of cockle shells and soft-shelled crabs. There were ragworms and starfish there too, which wriggled out of his fingers when he touched them. Once or twice he found something solid, only to pull out a tin can or a piece of junk. The rubbery sliminess of an old bike tyre made him pull back in alarm once, until he saw what it was and overcame his revulsion.

He searched there for at least an hour, success slipping away from him. If he had to leave it, there would not be a second go until late that night. There was no way he could search around in the mud when it was dark.

Whopper kept yelling at him from the dyke, but it was difficult to ascertain just what the old man wanted him to do. All Steve could see was a waving stick and the fact that Whopper peppered his instructions with oaths did not help.

He tried doing a systematic search of the area that Whopper seemed to want him to look within, but nothing came of it. The tide began to trickle in, over the mudflats and, when he dug a hole, water filled it instantly. It was becoming difficult to see where he had been already.

The salt water rippled over his dustbin-lid shoes and Steve knew he was going to have to get back to the dyke, or be trapped by the tide. On average, four or five people a year died in the creeks, through failure to judge the tides correctly. He did not want to end up a meal for the crabs.

Just when he was beginning to despair, his fingers touched a slim object. He felt around a little more, found it again, and pulled it out. It was the dagger! He held it up and gave a yell of triumph. Whopper waved his blackthorn.

Steve splodged back to Whopper and returned the dustbin lids, cleaning up in a bucketful of water on Whopper's boat. Then he ran home, the dagger safe in his pocket. Back in his bedroom he put the weapon in a plastic bowl in his cupboard. The rest of the household was beginning to stir and Steve pottered in his room, before going down to breakfast.

Gibbo was not on the bus. Someone said he was ill. Steve sat in his usual place, between Rosemary and

Graham. "I know what I've got to do now," he said. "I've been there. I know why it's important."

"You've been where?" asked Graham suspiciously.

Steve thought better of explaining. "Never mind," he said. "Rosemary, I've got the dagger back from the river. Now I've got to return it, to the place where I found it – that tomb on Kinder Scout. You must think how to help me."

"Tomb?" said Graham, going ashen.

"Don't be a wimp, Gray," said Rosemary. Then, "Well, what's your problem, Steve?"

"My problem is that I was lost up there. I don't know where to even start looking for the grave. All I can remember is that it's in a circle of stones – like standing stones only not squared off and not as high as Stonehenge."

"You mean, like Avebury?"

Steve recalled that particular school trip. "Yes, like Avebury. I've got to get that dagger back. The warrior can't survive in Ifurin without it. He needs his knife to fight the monsters he meets there. It's his only weapon. I suppose he would usually have been buried with a shield and spear, or sword or something; but this one has only got his dagger. I've got to get it back to him; put it in his hand, so that he owns it again, instead of me."

"Hand?" said Graham, shakily.

"Yes, the corpse had the dagger in its hand when I found it. You see I dug this shallow depression, like you're supposed to, so that I could be out of the wind, only I uncovered this arm holding the dagger. I peeled back the fingers of its hand – thinking it was a putrid old root – and . . ." Steve stopped.

It seemed that Graham was going to be sick.

Chapter Ten

The TV weatherman was predicting rain that night.

Steve sat in front of the screen, preoccupied with trying to think up ways of finding the warrior's burial plot on top of Kinder Scout. It seemed utterly hopeless. Even if Susan and Jack let him go to Derbyshire, how on earth would he find the grave? There was a whole moor to search and the terrain was not easy to cross. You couldn't just walk around looking for a set of stones. Of course, he might be lucky and stumble on them straight away, but the likelihood was he could spend weeks stamping around in peat bogs, in and out of the crevasses cut by the surface water. It was hopeless. Hopeless. It seemed he was going to spend the rest of his life being haunted by a ghost that left puddles all over the house.

Steve turned to look at his sister as she sat quietly sewing something in the armchair next to him. She looked tired these days, but Ben was enough to wear anyone out. Maybe it was a pleasant tiredness.

"How're you feeling, sis?"

She looked up and Jack took his eyes from the screen and stared at him too. "Feeling?"

Steve suddenly felt a little bit uncomfortable, a bit embarrassed. "I just thought you looked tired, that's all," he said, defensively.

Jack switched off the television set. Susan ran a hand through her hair. "I'm all right. Heavens, that's the first time you've thought of anyone but yourself in a long time. Aren't you worried about your spots any more?"

Steve turned away from her, angrily. "That's not fair," he said. She was right of course. He normally didn't bother with either of them. Jack and Susan had their lives to lead and he had his. That's how he had thought of it before, if he even bothered to think it.

Susan said softly, "You're right, it isn't fair. You think a lot of Benjy, and you help me."

"I do think of you two as well," he stuttered, red faced. "Honestly. It's just that my head's too full most of the time."

Susan nodded. "I keep forgetting what it's like to be your age. It's easy for me to say that those things I thought important at fourteen seem shallow now, but they were important then. I remember Mum saying to me, 'You have no worries at your age,' and thinking what a stupid statement. I had worries coming out of my ears: exams, my straight hair which I was not allowed to bob, the awful shoes she made me wear, the fact that Victor Jameson hardly knew I existed, the polio epidemic – I was so convinced I was going to catch it I lay awake in bed at nights, afraid. I had to keep wriggling my toes to convince myself that my legs weren't paralysed. And ghosts . . ."

Jack came in then, "Oh ghosts. I was terrified of ghosts. I used to creep into bed with my older brother at eight, but you can't do that at fourteen. You have to lie there and sweat."

"Did you ever see a ghost?" asked Steve, hopefully.

"Nope," said Jack. "I don't know that I really believed in such things, even then."

"Oh yes you did Jack, otherwise you wouldn't have been so scared," said Susan. "You can't say you lay there sweating and then in the next breath deny you believed in ghosts."

"I suppose not. Anyway, why are you asking, Steve? You worried about them?"

Steve was about to blurt out the whole story when there was a ring on the doorbell. Steve was so startled by the sound he almost hit the ceiling.

It was Mrs Densh from next door.

"I just looked out and saw you had washing still on the line, Sue. It's just started to spot with rain . . ."

"Oh, heavens, thanks Lila. I forgot to take it in before it got dark. I'll do it now."

"You sit down, I'll do it," said Jack, and he turned to Steve, "and you stop worrying about ghosts. Believe me, there's no such thing, not the kind you mean. The spirits that're left after the body dies, well they don't have any contact with this world. They have their own place. Your Mum and Dad – that's who you're worried about isn't it? – your parents are in another place. I don't know where it is and I can't prove it, but they wouldn't come back here – couldn't – and they certainly wouldn't do it to frighten their own son. I'll talk some more to you later, okay?"

"Okay."

When Jack had gone outside, Steve said goodnight to Susan and climbed the stairs. He went slowly, dreading what might be waiting for him in his bedroom.

He opened the door and switched on the light. The room was empty. Steve let out a sigh. Then he turned off the light and went to the window, looking out over the garden. In the glow from the living room and the open door, he could see Jack hastily taking washing from the line. Behind Jack, partially hidden by the hanging willow branches, was a dark shape. The dagger was back in the shed and the rain ghost was mooning over it.

Why hadn't Jack seen it? Why hadn't he sensed the warrior's presence, when Steve felt it so *strongly*, even from as far away as the bedroom? Adults: their spiritual nervous systems died when they reached a certain age. Jack could probably stare the ghost right in the face and still not know it was there. His brother-in-law was insensitive to the supernatural. Jack's head was full of things like bank statements, mortgages, paperwork, things to do with his job. People go blind, deaf and dumb to certain aspects of the world, once they take on responsibilities, thought Steve.

He pulled the curtains, undressed, got into his pyjamas, and climbed into bed. Suddenly, a thought struck him. The only time he had seen the ghost was when it was raining. It could get into the house, leave its damp patches in places, but it could not do so in its man shape. When it came inside, it probably drifted under doors or through keyholes as a cloud of mist, a cold vapour. Steve didn't mind that *so* much. It was still disturbing, but not so bad as a recognizable shape of a man.

While he lay in bed, restless, his problems grew to an enormous size. They were too large to solve and even thinking of Julie Parker could not drive them from his mind.

Several times he got up and stared out of the window. The ghost was still there, keeping its vigil over the garden shed. Whenever Steve looked out, the rain ghost looked up, or seemed to.

"I hope we have a dry summer," thought Steve, miserably. "I hope we a damn drought."

He finally fell asleep about midnight.

The following day was Saturday. Steve got up early and found his map of Kinder Scout. He pored over it for half an hour, trying to find any landmark even remotely like his standing stones. Some of the names, like Cluther Rocks, Madwoman's Stones or Seal Stones, might be what he was looking for, but could he find such places, even if he was allowed to go and look? Perhaps it was one of the more outlandish-sounding places, like Ringing Roger, Jaggers Clough or Noe Stool? But Steve knew from experience that the top of Kinder Scout was no easy territory. It was often covered with mist and, anyway, even the map said things like "Pennine Way Undefined" in places where the path crossed the moor.

Hopeless.

He left the house and went for a walk by the river. It was a bright morning, with no rain clouds in the sky. The poor old ghost was probably a puff of steam hanging around the shed. Poor old ghost? Yes, that's how he thought of the warrior now. Steve's experience in Ifurin was enough to turn some of his fear of the phantom into sympathy. How long could the warrior last in Ifurin without his weapon? Could he be killed again? Perhaps it was like that ancient Greek god, who was he – Poseidon? No, that was the one in

99

charge of the oceans. P – p – p . . . Trouble was, most of them seemed to begin with P. Pro – pro-something – Prometheus! That was it. He was chained to a rock by Zeus and had his liver eaten out by an eagle, every single day. Maybe the warrior in Ifurin was like Prometheus, and could be killed over and over again, never really dying but suffering the agony of death every time. That was terrible!

When he returned to the unmade road, Steve saw a figure coming towards him. It was Rosemary. She waved and smiled. "Steve Winston, this is your lucky day!"

Steve sighed. "You wouldn't think so to look at me, would you?"

Rosemary's round face was still beaming. "But I've solved your problem for you. You're going on a trip to Kinder Scout, in a month's time."

"What are you talking about?"

Rosemary took his arm and steered him back towards the river. "See, it's like this, buddy. While I was watching TV last night the announcer on Channel Four said that 'Treasure Hunt' – you know the Anneka Rice thing? –"

He nodded without interrupting her.

"–well, he said there was a new series coming in the autumn and that this time they wanted suggestions from the public as to the areas where the hunts should take place. I spent two hours trying to get through on the phone, but I finally did it!"

Something was beginning to seep through the murk that had clouded Steve's brain for the past few days. "You suggested somewhere?"

"Not only that," she gave his arm a squeeze, "they thought it was a good idea and they're going to do it. Wincey Willis, you know the lady who stays in the studio with Kenneth Kendall? She's the one who works out where the clues should be left. The woman who took my call rang me back and said. 'Wincey thinks Kinder Scout is a wonderful idea. Thank you, Rosemary, for your suggestion. A free Channel Four pen set will be sent to you by post.' "

"A free pen set?" The murk still hadn't cleared. Then he suddenly twigged. "Kinder Scout!"

"Right!" squealed Rosemary. "If you went with them, you could see the circle of stones from the air. It would be a doddle. Now all we've got to do is find out what day they're going to do it and you can stow away on the helicopter . . ."

Steve's spirits sank. "That's daft, Rosemary. How am I going to do that?"

She stopped and let go of his arm. The smile left her face. "Well, that's what I'd do," she said. "Haven't you got any sense of adventure?"

"I've got a sense of adventure, but I'm not potty. You can see how impossible it would be. There's no way I could manage to hide in a small helicopter without anyone seeing me, even if I *could* find the right one and climb aboard at the right time without anyone noticing. It's daft, Rosemary."

She nodded, grim faced. "You're right, it's daft. I'm romantic you know. I get these ideas and don't think them through. But we've still got Anneka's helicopter going over Kinder Scout. Why not write to her and ask her if you can go with them?"

"What, like 'Jim'll Fix It'? But what excuse will I give. I can't tell them I'm going to give a dagger back to a corpse, can I?"

"No, but you can say you lost the locket given to you by your mother on her death bed, that you promised you would keep it always, and that you

101

can't sleep now because of that promise. You can tell them you were lost up on Kinder, that they didn't expect to find you alive, but you survived because you held your mother's locket and thought of her. Tell them you lost the locket by the standing stones and you would only recognize the spot from the air."

"And what happens when they drop me there and I come back empty handed?"

Rosemary smiled. "You won't. You'll have your mother's locket in your hand and you'll show it to them."

Steve almost shouted, "But I haven't got my mother's damn locket!" Instead, he said it quietly.

Rosemary reached up with both hands and felt behind her neck. A moment later she dropped something in Steve's hand. It was a small gold locket.

"It's antique," she said. "It was my grandmother's. You can borrow it for Operation Kinder Scout. Don't lose it, will you?"

"Rosemary," said Steve, when he could find the words, "you're a damn genius. An *evil* genius – I've got to lie through my teeth to a lot of people – but a genius, just the same." He gave her a quick squeeze and her smile disappeared, to be replaced by a funny look.

He wondered if she was embarrassed because he was being demonstrative and he said, "Didn't mean to hug you. I just got excited."

She looked away, over the river. "That's all right," she said, in a quiet voice. "I didn't mind." Then she turned back, and cried in a brisk tone, "Well, who's going to ring them up? I'll do it. You'll only stumble over your words and end up blurting out the truth. The trouble is, no one's going to believe the truth."

"I dunno about this story we've made up," said Steve, getting worried again.

"Look, it's not going to harm anyone. Lies are only bad if they're malicious. As my dad always says, 'why spoil a good story with the truth?' We're not going to hurt anyone. We're trying to help your ghost warrior."

"That's true." He thought of something else. "But my sister? She knows my mother didn't leave me a locket. What can I say to her?"

"I don't know. It's up to you. I don't mind ringing Channel Four again, if you want to give it a try."

"Let me think about it," said Steve.

Once he was back at the house, Steve made a sudden decision. He would call Julie Parker. He would tell Julie all that had happened, she would sympathize with him, and perhaps suggest some alternative to Rosemary's scheme. Julie had come to visit him, after all, when he was recovering from his ordeal on Kinder. In this way he could kill two birds with one stone. He could share his problem with Julie and have her concerned for his welfare, and perhaps she could suggest a way of returning the dagger not as dramatic as Rosemary's plan. A more sensible idea.

He picked up the telephone and dialled.

"Hello? Mrs Parker? Could I speak to Julie please? This is Steve – Steven Winston, one of her school-friends. Oh, she's *spoken* about me? Thanks. Yes, thanks."

A short wait, then, "Julie? Steve . . . what? Oh, Steve *Winston*. Yes. Listen . . ." and he launched into his problem.

Afterwards, he sat and stared at the phone. Unbelievable!

"Well, thank *you* Miss Julie-damn-Stephanie

Parker for your advice. A psychiatrist is the *last* person I want to see at the moment, thank-you-very-much, Miss Fishgut, Ratfink, Weaselbrain Parker. Chuhh! 'See a shrink', " he mimicked in a falsetto voice.

Susan came into the room. "Pardon?" she said, hoiking Benjamin from one hip to the other.

"Nothing," said Steve, glowering. "Just talking to myself."

That afternoon Steve was caught out in a freak shower. The ghost dogged his footsteps all the way home, drifting around him. When he got near to the front door, the warrior passed right through him, soaking him to the skin with freezing rain. During the brief contact he caught a taste of the ghost's own terrors, which were alarmingly alien. Steve had never before experienced fear of that depth or strangeness. He did not understand them. They were fears that had little meaning in a modern world. They were the terrors of a man whose world is a small, mean place full of life magic and death magic and absolute belief in both. They were the fears of a primitive rain worshipper, whose knowledge of the world came from his shaman; his warrior-king-priest, who used men's ignorance to keep them powerless.

Steve felt the rain ghost's horror. It was a dark dread of shade and shadow, rock, tree and hill. It was an ugly reverence of a dream world more terrifying and more real than a bloodletting on a midnight moor. In his head there were drums beating frightening rhythms and gutteral voices describing unimaginable tortures in an underworld full of demons.

When he got into the living room, Susan said, "Who was that?"

104

He shivered, dripping on to the carpet. "Who was who?"

She looked up. "I was watching through the window. I thought I saw someone with you."

"Shadow," said Steve. "You must have seen the shadow of something. Maybe it was the trees? I sometimes see things that look like other things," he gabbled, "especially when the light's funny, like in the late evening or early morning . . ."

"Stevie! You're soaking."

It stopped his chatter and he realized he was not only dripping on to the carpet, but shaking drops all over the newspaper which Jack had left on the floor.

"Yeah, sorry sis. Got caught. I'll go and change."

That evening he ran round to Rosemary's house and hammered on her door. Luckily she was the one who answered, though Steve could hear her father asking who was knocking the house down.

"Hi!" said Rosemary, brightly.

"Do it!" was Steve's hoarse reply.

Chapter Eleven

Rosemary stood before him in the doorway and shook her head slowly. "I've thought about it some more," she said, "and I can't do it."

She looked tight lipped and firm as a house. Steve was stunned. Rosemary had seemed so willing to help him before, and now she was going back on it, just when he needed her most. What had he done? What had he said? He must have upset her in some way, for her to reject him like this. Perhaps she had found out that he had called Julie Parker first? Maybe Julie-damn-Stephanie Parker had split on him?

"What? You're not going to help me?" he croaked.

She stepped outside and closed the door behind her. "Yes, I'm going to help you, but we've got to do this straight. I realized after I got home that if we used my elaborate plan, we'd be bound to slip up somewhere along the line. Can you imagine how difficult it would be, keeping a straight face when someone from the TV rings up your sister to ask if it's okay? Let's go to Jack and Susan explain to them what you want to do and why. *Then* I'll call Channel Four."

Steve felt utterly depressed. Although he thought the world of his sister and brother-in-law, Steve recognized that when it came down to the bottom line they were quite rigid about certain things. Steve could show them the ghost of course, but he knew what Jack would do. Once Jack was able to accept that Steve was being haunted by a supernatural being, he would call a priest to exorcise the creature. Jack believed in science and experts. If you had a ghost, then you got rid of it in a scientific way. You called an expert in paranormal happenings, an exorcist, a ghostbuster. You didn't mess around with it yourself, no matter how much you thought you knew about the reasons for the ghost's presence.

"It won't work," he said. "They'll only get us in deeper."

"We don't have to tell them the whole truth," said Rosemary, stepping out briskly towards Steve's house while he dragged on behind. "That's not the same as telling them a lie. What we say is that you robbed a grave, you've been having bad dreams about it and now you feel guilty. You have to replace the item. Come on."

He caught up with her, still full of misgivings.

When Rosemary had finished explaining to Jack and Susan there was silence. Both adults were looking at Steve. "He has been a wreck lately," Susan said.

Steve muttered, "Thanks a lot, sis."

Jack picked up the dagger which was on the table in front of them. "This should really go to a museum or something," he said.

Rosemary retorted, "Jack, museums have got

107

hundreds of rusty old knives which no one looks at. This is important to Steve. He took something – by accident because he didn't know it was a grave – and he wants to put it back. He feels he's desecrated a sacred place."

Susan intervened. "Rosemary's right, Jack. We've all been brainwashed into thinking that *every* historical object that's found belongs under glass, to be stared at by the public. Some things should be left where they're placed by their original owners, especially the contents of graves. How would you like it if someone dug up your mother, took her wedding ring and put it in a museum in New York or Frankfurt or somewhere, for the tourists to gawp at?"

"It's not the same thing . . ." Jack began, but Rosemary interrupted.

"It's *exactly* the same thing, Jack."

Seeing that everyone was ranged against him, Jack eventually relented, but asked that he be allowed to make the arrangements. He said he appreciated Rosemary's offer to ring Channel Four, but he felt it was his duty to do these things.

Susan said to Rosemary, "It's this *man* thing. Let him do it or he'll get upset."

Rosemary laughed. "All right."

Steve was happy to let *anyone* do it.

Jack called Channel Four and was eventually put through to the producer of "Treasure Hunt" who took more than a little persuading. Jack said that he realized this was an unusual request, but the situation was unusual in itself. He pointed out that though the programme was popular, this favour could do it no harm. The producer saw the wisdom in that remark. He would get back to Jack within a couple of days.

★   ★   ★

In fact the producer telephoned the very next day.

"You're on!" said Jack to Steve, after he had put down the phone. "Three weeks from Saturday. I've got to get you to the car park below Kinder Scout. We're supposed to keep this a secret from everyone." He paused and puffed out his chest. "This is quite a responsibility, isn't it? An important event. I mean . . ."

Sue raised her eyes to the ceiling and handed Benjamin to him. "Pongo-pongo-pongo," she said.

Jack said, "Heck, Benjy," holding his nose.

Steve, catching a whiff of Ben's latest devastating attack on the clean air zones of East Anglia, left the room quickly. He wondered how long it would be before Friends of the Earth or Greenpeace got wind of Benjy's disregard for the pollution problems of Great Britain and began campaigning for his deportation.

Somehow Steve struggled through the next three weeks. Although the rain ghost didn't appear, Steve could feel its presence. It was as if the warrior knew that a scheme had been formed to return its precious weapon to its possession. There was a kind-of patience in the air, along with that terrible sense of melancholy.

By the time the Saturday came, Steve was almost sorry that he and his ancient spiritual warrior were to be parted. They had got used to one another. The rain ghost made Steve feel different, as if he had a special relationship with a wild exotic beast that had escaped from the zoo. Its presence had also helped Steve think more about his dead parents. Previously he had always kept them out of his thoughts, the memory of their leaving being too painful. Now, he began to remember some of the good times he had had with them.

Jack drove Steve to Derbyshire and they arrived at the car park below Kinder Scout to find a man from the National Trust waiting for them. Later, amidst great noise and swirling dust, the helicopter arrived. A pretty blonde woman in a black jumpsuit leapt from the machine and came running over to the car, a broad smile on her face. "Steven?" she said, "I'm Anneka Rice."

"I know," he said, overawed for the moment.

"Come on then," she cried, grabbing his hand and pulling him towards the waiting helicopter, "we've got to rush. I've found the clue. Wincey's stopped the clock."

"Won't *I* be on TV?" he shouted over the noise of the helicopter.

"Nope," she smiled, "not unless you're in one of the adverts."

Steve was a little disappointed, but he recalled why he was there. It was not to star in a TV programme, but to put something right.

Anneka had so much energy, enthusiasm and bounce that she made Steve feel breathless just to watch her. She told him to sit behind her seat, next to the cameraman. He did as he was asked. Then she cried, "Let's go Keith. Up to the top again. Steve wants to have a quick look around the moor."

The helicopter rose and flashed along above Griod's Brook, to the plateau. Steve could see walkers along the track staring up at him and pointing.

"Kenneth," Anneka was saying into her mike, "we've got Steve with us now. Just going – wheeee – what a view! Can you see it? Super view. There's

Madwoman's Stones down there. Wonder why they call it that? Somebody got lost up here I suppose and went crazy. I know I would. Oh, Keith's doing a circuit now . . ."

She turned. "Okay Steve. Tell us when you see the spot."

Steve stared down at the ground. It all looked so different from the air. How on earth was he going to recognize his little circle of stones? But then the pilot, Keith Thompson, took them lower and zoomed around just above the moor. Steve concentrated, trying to recognize landmarks and guess where he had been the night he was lost. Anneka bubbled, "Just tell us when, Steve. We haven't got long remember." She gave him another one of her lovely broad smiles and he smiled back.

Suddenly he saw something – a rock formation – which might have been the tower that he had sat under for some time that night. He asked Keith Thompson to go back over it again, approaching it from the front so that he could get a better view of it. The pilot obliged.

Steve was certain that was the rock tower.

He glanced over the moor around the tower. He couldn't have walked very far that night, in the dark and mist. The ground was rugged, full of crazed channels where the raw peat showed through, black. Steve begged for one more circuit around the tower.

The pilot did as requested and finally Steve saw them.

"There they are! That's the place!"

Anneka asked Keith to land as close as possible to the site and the helicopter pilot again obliged, putting Steve down next to the tower. Anneka said, "Shall I come with you?" but Steve shook his head.

111

He leapt down from the chopper and ran across the spongy ground, stumbling occasionally on mounds of grass.

A chill wind sprang up as he searched the horizon for his ring of waist-high monoliths. There was a sense of loneliness touching his spirit. He was isolated once again, from the rest of civilization. The helicopter was behind him somewhere and around him the peat moor stretched, cold and hostile. Steve had to fight the urge to run back to those people waiting for him in their modern machine. Instead, he forced himself onward, over the primeval landscape where ground mists slid like flattened snakes around the tussocks and clumps.

Once, he fell into a cleft in the peat, and scrambled out, the fear rising in his throat like vomit. He was afraid of touching things. The task he had ahead of him was now filling his head with all kinds of terrible thoughts. He had to take the dead hand of a primitive warrior and place the dagger in its cold bony fingers. Inside Steve's heart, it was winter.

It was quite different from the first time. When he had taken the weapon, he had thought he was clutching a root. Now he knew he was going to have to grapple with a corpse. He could feel the animosity of this brooding landscape, far from the regular track used by walkers. He was an intruder, unwanted, and he knew the bog would not hesitate to suck him to a black gruesome death if it had the chance.

It was hiding the small circle of stones from him, throwing up hummocks to block his view. *Please, please let me find it soon!* thought Steve. How had he stayed a night in this place and come out sane? Impossible. He felt the soul of this dark and dismal moor and it was a mad place. *Madwoman's Stones*. He knew what had sent her crazy: the secrets of the moor got inside you, festered, drove you out of your mind.

Finally, he reached the circle of stones and gave out a huge sob of relief. He saw the arm protruding just a couple of inches above the surface. How could he have mistaken it for a root? He could see the claw-like fingers now, as plain as anything.

His heart was racing ahead of him, eager to be on the way back to the helicopter. Swallowing hard, he squeezed between two stones and kneeled by the corpse. Gingerly, he reached down to place the dagger in the dead man's grip, closing the fingers for him.

They seemed to close easily, almost of their own accord.

Revolted, Steve jerked backwards. The dagger remained in the clutches of the warrior, but Steve's work was still not finished, though he was reluctant to touch the mummified arm he knew what he had to do.

Overcoming his squeamishness, he took the exposed arm with both hands and pressed it back down into the peat, watching the oily water close over it as the soggy ground swallowed up the limb. Steve then grabbed some loose peat and filled in the depression he had made the night he was lost, until he was sure the warrior's arm was covered, hidden, and would not spring up again. To be absolutely certain, he put his shoulder behind a large, precariously-balanced standing stone and pushed it flat on to the tomb. It would take a crane to lift the now horizontal monolith. The warrior was safe for all time.

\ "Cheers pal," said Steve irreverently. Relief surged through him. A feeling of lightness entered him and he knew he had completed his task to the satisfaction of the rain ghost. He felt there should be some fireworks: some tremendous pyrotechnical display which would light up the whole plateau. After all, it was a momentous occasion. The ancient tribesman was once again armed and ready for his adventures in Ifurin. The balance had been restored.

Instead, the wind soughed through the gaps in the standing stones and away to the west some sheep chomped on marsh grass. There was to be no demonstration of the transference of power. It was a discreet occasion, devoid of violence of any kind. However, Steve did notice with a little satisfaction that some rather black clouds were drifting in, over the mountain. Perhaps the gods would mark the occasion later on in the day, with their own firework display?

He ran back to the waiting chopper.

"Okay?" shouted Anneka. Steve nodded, and climbed aboard.

The helicopter flew vertically upwards. Steve got a last glimpse of the rain warrior's grave, and then they peeled away, towards the edge of the plateau.

In the car park, Anneka delivered Steve back to Jack, who shook her hand warmly and thanked her and the Treasure Hunt team for all their help. She laughed, said it was a pleasure and, with her hair streaming behind her, ran back to begin the hunt for the next clue. Steve sighed as they drove away. Anneka Rice was a very beautiful woman and, when he came to think about it, Rosemary was a lot like her.

When they got home, it was raining.

Steve got out of the car, exhausted from the trip. He needed the relief of sleep. He walked down the pathway, towards the house. There was a light on in the living room, which looked comforting. He could see Sue and Rosemary in there.

As he passed the garden shed, he glanced in the direction of the willow tree. He almost swallowed his tongue in fright. There was a black sinister shape, hiding amongst the curtain of branches.

Oh no! he thought. *Please, no!*

Jack's footsteps were close behind him and his brother-in-law almost ran into the back of him. "What are you . . ." began Jack. Then he stopped to peer through the rain, at the willow. "Who's that?"

Steve began, miserably, "It's . . ."

The shape came through the leafy curtain and confronted them. "It's me Jack, Whopper. I got caught out in this 'ere rain. Just shelterin' under your ole willer, if that's all right."

Steve recognized the cauliflower nose and he almost yelled in delight.

Jack said, "Come on indoors, Whopper, till it stops."

"No, no," replied the old man. Steve knew Whopper had a terrible fear of cosy family life and warm comfortable homes, thinking they might be catching, like some dread disease. "I'll get on, thankee."

They watched him shuffle away to his independence on the rotting boat he called home.

Chapter Twelve

Steve, dressed in jeans and *Ray Bees* T-shirt, was standing by the gate waiting for his sister to emerge from the house. It was early morning. He had a day off school while some urgent maintenance was being carried out on the building.

The local smuggler was passing the gate.

Jack came out of the house, two minutes late for work.

Whopper tried to dodge out of the way of Jack as Steve's brother-in-law came hurling through the garden gateway, cornflakes in hand. But Whopper had neither the youth nor the constitution of an American football player, and failed. Warm milk splashed on his bulbous, lumpy nose. He wiped it away with the greasy sleeve of his jacket as Jack dashed past yelling, "Sorry Whopper!"

Steve came out and leaned on the gate. "He's still practising for the Olympics."

"Ar," replied Whopper, "I'll practise 'im, next

time. He'll been goin' in for the high jump afore he's much older."

With that, the old smuggler shuffled off along the road to the dyke grumbling away to himself.

Gibbo hurried by next. Although still very wary of Steve he gave the traditional local greeting. "Wuppa Winston."

"Wuppa Gibson."

Both boys were cautious in one another's presence. Steve still couldn't be sure that the tough farm boy was not suddenly going to leap on him and pummel him to the ground. On the other hand he knew that Gibbo had been so shaken by the rain ghost that the youth had decided to keep their encounters to a minimum. That was fine by Steve.

Susan came out of the house with Benjamin in a pushchair.

"Ya!" yelled Ben, opening his arms as if to enfold and cuddle the wonderful summer morning.

Steve took over wheeling the pushchair and the trio set off down the lane. There was the smell of hot grasses in the air and the crickets were filling the hedgerow with dry noises. It was a smouldering morning: the kind of summer day that everyone remembers for the rest of their lives. There were birds in sky, on the ground, in the trees, and things rustled amongst the papery weeds of the ditch.

Benjamin was quick to point out various sights of interest, like the tractor in the field, or the pheasant running along the hedgerow. "Ya!" he cried, his chubby little finger waving in the general direction of the object, and his mouth would drop open with the sheer magnificence of the event. Everything and anything that moved, made a noise, or just looked interesting, was of wondrous significance to Ben.

It was a long walk to Ashingdon Minster, where Steve's parents were buried, but they eventually reached the eleventh-century church built by King Canute after his defeat of Edmund Ironside.

Susan took the garden shears from the basket under the pushchair and began clipping the tall grass around the grave. Steve generally tidied up and picked some wild flowers to place on the tomb. It was the first time the pair of them had been back to the church since their parents' funeral.

Suddenly, Steve was aware of a figure looming over him, as he knelt by the stone that bore his father's and mother's names. The shadow startled him, and he looked up, shielding his eyes.

It was the vicar. "Hello, you've come to tend the grave?"

Susan paused in her work. "Yes, we should have done it before . . . but we've only just got round to it."

"Fine," said the vicar. He tickled Benjamin under the chin and narrowly missed having the impression of two front teeth in his finger.

Looking at the stone, he said, "The Winstons? Sad accident."

"Our mum and dad," said Steve.

The vicar murmured something conciliatory, saying he had known Steve's parents. "Nice couple," he remarked. "Well liked. Respected."

When he had gone, Susan said, "Well liked, but a bit wild – I shouldn't have thought Mum and Dad were respected. Not in the way he meant. Mother was never very mumsy, and Dad liked parties and betting on the dogs."

"Was he a boozer?" said Steve.

Susan frowned. "Not exactly. He liked a drink, so did Mum, but they weren't drunk all the time. They just liked to enjoy themselves – extroverts, you know – they liked company, and you must remember Dad playing jazz on the piano, and Mum's tap dancing routine. She used to dance on the living-room table when she'd had a few, and Dad would do that trick where he pretended to swallow a balloon and prick the bulge under his jumper, making believe he had burst his stomach."

"I remember that," said Steve, recalling times when he had been disturbed of an evening and had gone to the top of stairs and looked down at a party in progress in his parents' living room. He had seen his mother doing her party piece once, and his dad doing the balloon joke a couple of times.

"Nothing wrong with that," he said.

"No, of course not. They were good to us, you know."

"I know," said Steve, staring down at the names that meant nothing to him. If the grave had said MUM AND DAD it would have meant much more to him than REBECCA ANN WINSTON or ROGER PETER WINSTON. He didn't know those formal people, with proper names. Even BECKY AND RODGE would have been better. Becky and Rodge were the couple who lived on the Ashingdon Road, who were such cheerful beggars they made you wince on a grey dismal winter's morning when you wanted to be miserable for a while.

That evening Graham called round and asked Steve if he wanted to go to the cinema in Southend. It was a silly question: Steve always wanted to go to the cinema. Like Graham he was a film buff.

Once outside the house, Graham said in an American accent, "Listen kid, we got two broads comin' with us."

"What?"

Graham reverted to his normal voice. His eyes shone behind his glasses. "Girls; Rosemary and Julie Parker."

Steve allowed this to sink in. "Julie Parker," he said, flatly.

"Yeah. We're sort of – we're sort of going out together," said Graham. "I asked her out to the pictures and she said yes, if you and Rosemary would come too."

"And Rosemary?"

"She's agreed. She didn't mind. Good old Rosemary."

"Yeah," said Steve. "Good old Rosemary."

"By the way," said Graham, "Jack's spoken to Dad about our phone bill. He said he'd pay it for him. Dad tried to say no, but Jack insisted."

"Good old Jack," said Steve.

"Yeah, good old Jack."

The journey by bus was a little subdued with everyone sitting in awkward silence. Rosemary tried to get the conversation going a bit, saying, "Canoe race next week. Bet Graham wins," but they were all a little too aware of the change in their circumstances. Three of them had been to pictures together before, many times, but that was before these strange barriers had grown between them. Steve felt that things could never be the same again. They seemed to have lost something: a childhood friendship, though Steve had not thought of himself as a kid since he had turned twelve. When you got to that age, kids were bewildered First Years, who didn't know which from what. He felt a bit sad, a little bereft. Something had gone, without even so much as sounding a bell, or flying a flag.

There were compensations for their lost comrade-ship though. In the cinema, once the picture had started, Rosemary reached across the arm of the seat and her slim hand slipped into his own. When he dared to look at her, she gave him a little smile. Steve's blood turned to warm milk. He gave the soft fingers a gentle squeeze. Suddenly, he felt sorry for his pal Graham, stuck with Julie Parker.

point® THRILLERS

Read them and *scream!*

☐ MC44330-5	**The Accident** Diane Hoh	$2.95
☐ MC43115-3	**April Fools** Richie Tankersley Cusick	$2.95
☐ MC44236-8	**The Baby-sitter** R.L. Stine	$2.95
☐ MC44332-1	**The Baby-sitter II** R.L. Stine	$3.25
☐ MC43278-8	**Beach Party** R.L. Stine	$2.95
☐ MC43125-0	**Blind Date** R.L. Stine	$2.75
☐ MC43279-6	**The Boyfriend** R.L. Stine	$2.95
☐ MC44316-X	**The Cheerleader** Caroline B. Cooney	$2.95
☐ MC44884-6	**The Return of the Vampire** Caroline B. Cooney	$2.95
☐ MC43291-5	**Final Exam** A. Bates	$2.95
☐ MC41641-3	**The Fire** Caroline B. Cooney	$2.95
☐ MC43806-9	**The Fog** Caroline B. Cooney	$2.95
☐ MC43050-5	**Funhouse** Diane Hoh	$2.95
☐ MC44333-0	**The Girlfriend** R.L. Stine	$3.25
☐ MC44904-4	**The Invitation** Diane Hoh	$2.95
☐ MC43203-6	**The Lifeguard** Richie Tankersley Cusick	$2.75
☐ MC44582-0	**Mother's Helper** A. Bates	$2.95
☐ MC44768-8	**My Secret Admirer** Carol Ellis	$2.75
☐ MC44238-4	**Party Line** A. Bates	$2.95
☐ MC44237-6	**Prom Dress** Lael Littke	$2.95
☐ MC44941-9	**Sister Dearest** D.E. Athkins	$2.95
☐ MC43014-9	**Slumber Party** Christopher Pike	$2.75
☐ MC41640-5	**The Snow** Christopher Pike	$2.75
☐ MC43280-X	**The Snowman** R.L. Stine	$2.95
☐ MC43114-5	**Teacher's Pet** Richie Tankersley Cusick	$2.95
☐ MC43742-9	**Thirteen** Edited by Tonya Pines	$3.25
☐ MC44235-X	**Trick or Treat** Richie Tankersley Cusick	$2.95
☐ MC43139-0	**Twisted** R.L. Stine	$2.75
☐ MC44256-2	**Weekend** Christopher Pike	$2.95
☐ MC44916-8	**The Window** Carol Ellis	$2.95

Available wherever you buy books, or use this order form.